Spies on the Devil's Belt

Betsy Haynes

Illustrated by Mort Küntsler

AN
APPLE
PAPERBACK

SCHOLASTIC INC.
New York Toronto London Auckland Sydney

ISBN 0-590-40567-5

Copyright © 1974 by Betsy Haynes. All rights reserved. Published by Scholastic Inc., 730 Broadway, New York, NY 10003, by arrangement with Lodestar Books, a division of E.P. Dutton. APPLE PAPERBACK is a registered trademark of Scholastic Inc.

12 11 10 9 8 7 6 5 4 3 2 1   1   0 1 2 3 4 5/9

Printed in the U.S.A.   11

For my son Craig
who wanted this to be
a story about lizards

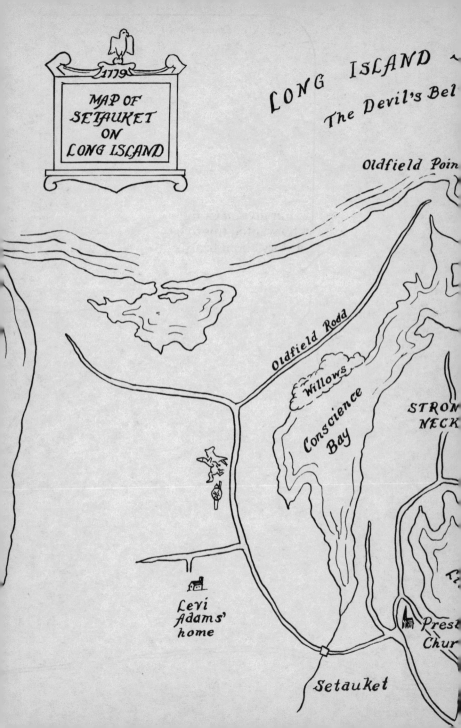

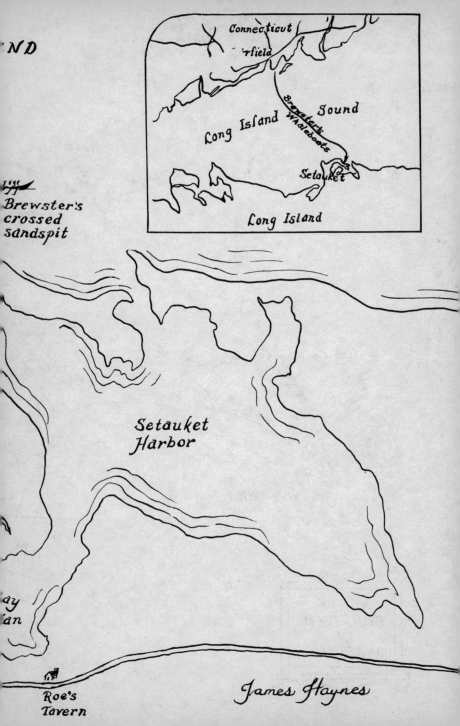

N D

Connecticut

rfield

Long Island   Sound

Brewster's
Whaleboats

Setauket

Long Island

Brewster's
crossed
sandspit

Setauket
Harbor

ay
ian

Roe's
Tavern

James Haynes

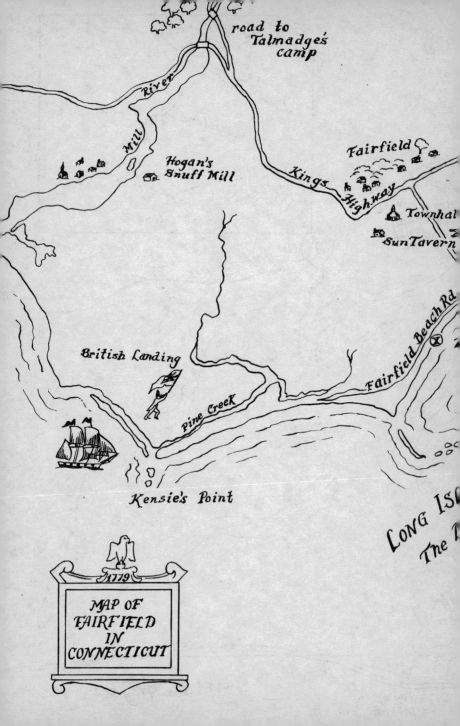

road to
Talmadge's
camp

River

Mill

Fairfield

Hogan's
Snuff Mill

Kings
Highway

Townhall

Sun Tavern

Fairfield Beach Rd.

British Landing

Fairfield

Pine Creek

Kensie's Point

LONG ISL
The I

1779

MAP OF
FAIRFIELD
IN
CONNECTICUT

Ash Creek

Penfield's
Tide Mill

Black
Rock
Fort

Black
Rock
Harbor

SOUND

; Belt

Connecticut

Fairfield

Sound

Long Island

Brewster's
Whaleboats

Setauket

Long Island

James Haynes

Chapter 1

They trudged up the naked hill like a parade of sleepwalkers; twelve men, two abreast, leaning into the rain, each man carrying a narrow wooden plank in each hand. The May rain that was falling from a pewter sky showed no signs of letting up, and the curled brims of the men's three-cornered hats funneled the water like porch gutters. At the crest of the hill the solemn formation turned to face the tiny hamlet of Fairfield, Connecticut, which lay below. Then on a signal from one of them the men raised the boards above their heads and began clapping them together in slowly measured time.

The heavy cadence rolled across fragrant apple orchards, spanned streams and fieldstone fences, sped over freshly plowed fields, and pierced the clapboard walls and shingled roofs of every house for miles around.

Jonathan Barlowe watched the men from behind a clump of paper birch trees near the base of the great hill and absently drummed his fingertips against the white bark in time with the clapping of the boards. He would have to hurry now because soon the people would come.

Jonathan hoisted a knapsack onto his back, picked up the smoothbore Brown Bess that lay at his feet in the sodden grass, and hurried toward the road. Although slightly built for fourteen, he was uncommonly strong, and he leaped over a felled log with ease even though he carried everything he owned in the world with him. The heavy rain gathered in his curly brown hair, which was pulled together into an unruly club at the back of his neck, and rolled in rivulets down his face and into his eyes, finally converging to follow the deep cleft in his chin and pour down his chest as one steady stream.

The road was still deserted, but he knew that soon it would be filled with townspeople. Jonathan quickened his pace, stopping only once to break a heavily flowered branch off a dogwood tree near the road, and arrived at the empty churchyard panting for breath.

A dozen or so birds huddled together in the empty belfry of the church, and beneath the stately spire the door stood open. Jonathan saw no one about, but still he ducked low as he went past the windows and hurried around behind the church to where rows of marble gravestones glistened like pearls in the rain.

Jonathan stopped at the graveyard's entrance and took a deep breath. His heart fluttered inside his chest like a frightened bird. He had hurried, but now that he was here he wished that he had not. Perhaps he could have waited one more day. He should have fixed the Gladdens' fence to further repay them for their kindness during his father's long illness and for giving him food and a place to sleep these ten days since his father died.

No. He had made up his mind. He would say a final good-bye to his father and be on his way quickly and quietly before anyone could persuade him to stay.

Abruptly the clapping stopped. There would little time left to be alone. He made his way to the back of the cemetery to where the modest stones were made of red sandstone and the grave plots were small and close together, and stopped beside a grave where the bare ground was mounded high in spite of the pounding rain. Placing the dogwood branch beside the headstone, Jonathan knelt by the grave. He reached out and gently touched the freshly carved words on the stone.

NATHANIEL BARLOWE

Born August 17, 1738   Died May 24, 1779

Jonathan blinked away the tears that filled his eyes. It hurt now to remember how he had longed to be on his own, to be free. As the son of a widowed itinerant tailor, he had traveled the countryside in a cramped and rickety wagon, helping his father measure and cut cloth and card thread. At night he had fallen asleep watching his father's eyes swell shut from the strain as he stitched by candlelight.

But that was not all that Jonathan had watched as he traveled. He had seen boys with willow poles angling for sunnies in glistening streams. He had watched boys jumping from haylofts and racing bareback through winnowing meadow grass. Once he had seen a pair of boys his own age running through a field of wild asparagus and scattering a flock of grouse in every direction, and he had pretended for a while that he was running with them and that he would come home that night to a house with a soft featherbed.

His father had not understood these longings, perhaps because he had not had the time to listen. Sometimes Jonathan talked it over with Stony and Dover, the ancient team that pulled the wagon, but now they had been sold along with the wagon and its bolts of cloth, its spools, spindles, and needles, to pay the small debts his father had left and to buy the coffin and headstone.

Jonathan stood up slowly. I'm on my own now, he thought. Free and independent . . . alone. He shivered in the cold rain and watched the heavy drops beat the snow-white petals of the dogwood into the mud, leaving the once beautiful bough stripped and forlorn.

A horse neighed in the churchyard. Jonathan's pulse quickened. He was not completely alone. The people were beginning to come. He would stay out of sight and not join them, but he would listen and watch through the window until this loneliness passed. Then he would be on his way.

He stowed his knapsack and musket behind his father's gravestone and sat down again to wait. No one would notice him here. Folding his arms across his knees and resting his head, Jonathan listened to the creak and groan of wagons pulling into the churchyard and to the sound of men and women calling out greetings to one another. After a while all was quiet. The people had gone inside the church. The meeting had begun.

Staying low, Jonathan crept to the nearest window, cautiously raised his head until his eyes were above the sill, and looked inside. Men milled around in the aisles, and women chatted together over the backs of the pews while their children wiggled uncomfortably in the seats beside them. The pulpit was still empty. Whomever the people were expecting had not arrived yet.

Jonathan moved away from the window with a sigh. The rain, which had begun as a storm the night before, had all but stopped. There was no reason to stay any longer.

From a distance came the sound of horses' hooves, faint at first, then coming closer at a gallop. Jonathan flattened himself against the side of the church and peered around the corner of the building toward the road. The two riders who approached at high speed were haloed in spray as their thundering horses stamped across the rain-soaked ground to stop short at the front steps of the church.

The door burst open and a man rushed out. "Captain Brewster. Welcome! Here, let me take care of your horses," he said.

Jonathan and his father had been virtually untouched by America's war for independence, and his father had carefully tailored his political leanings to fit the leanings of those for whom he was stitching a coat. Nevertheless, Jonathan had heard stories of the illustrious Captain Caleb Brewster of the Continental Artillery, whose tiny fleet of whaleboats crisscrossed Long Island Sound and fearlessly raided enemy garrisons near Setauket, Long Island.

He hurried back to the window in time to see the captain stride into the room. His companion, a lank, long-nosed sailor with a knit cap pulled low on his forehead, remained near the door as Brewster headed straight for the pulpit.

Jonathan could not recall ever having seen such a giant of a man. Cannonball fists hammered the air in time with his step, and water droplets glistened like stars in the midnight black of his shaggy hair and full beard. The blue coat faced with scarlet that was the uniform of the artilleryman fit tautly across his massive shoulders.

Brewster turned sharply with an agility not common to such big men and surveyed his audience with piercing eyes. "I am here today for two reasons," he began. His voice was commanding, and Jonathan had no difficulty distinguishing the words through the thick windowpane. "First, I want to thank you for the sacrifices that you've already made."

There was a stirring among the people, many of whom smiled or nodded, and Caleb Brewster gestured for quiet before going on. "I'm proud to be able to say that I live in Fairfield, because you've shared your livestock, your crops, and your warm clothing with my men, mostly by doing without yourself. You've even given your church bell to be melted down for cannon."

He nodded appreciatively toward the twelve men sitting in a row on the deacon's pew, whose clapping boards had called the people together.

"But there's a second reason why I'm here today," he continued. "I'm afraid that I have to ask you to give more. I need men. I need men who'll be cold and hungry and scared. Men who'll ride the rolls and swells in a rowboat and learn firsthand why Long Island Sound is called the Devil's Belt. I need men who put freedom and liberty above home and family. Men who can't live under tyranny. And, my friends and neighbors, I need them today!" These last words thundered forth like cannon fire and charged the air with an almost tangible force, pinning the men and women to their seats in stunned silence.

Suddenly near the back of the room a short, wiry man sprang to his feet. "What do you mean, give more?" he demanded. "We have our own fort at Black Rock to man and supply and a home guard of twenty-six men to maintain. You've already taken nearly half your crew from the husbands and fathers of Fairfield. Good grief, man, how can you ask for more?"

All eyes turned to the captain, who regarded the man narrowly. Then he spoke again in a voice thick with disgust. "The British government is driving us to poverty with taxes, money that they steal from us and carry across the sea to fatten themselves. They govern us with laws made by men who've never even seen our land."

Brewster paused as if to regain control. When he

spoke again, his voice was a low rumble beneath blazing eyes. "Joshua Claybourne, there are certain things that every human being has a need for. A need for food. A need for sleep. A need for love. And the chance to live in freedom and dignity. You said, how dare I ask. I guess I made a bad choice of words. I don't ask. I don't beg. I don't even demand. I *challenge* you to serve yourself!" He added the punctuation of silence to his words, letting them sink into the minds and hearts of his audience before he stepped down from the pulpit.

"I'll be at the Sun Tavern to take your enlistments," he said. Then he strode up the aisle toward the door slightly slower than he had come in.

Jonathan stood outside the window, filled with the words he had just heard. Freedom. Liberty. To answer to no one. To make your own rules. Your country and yourself, both striving for the same things. The thought made him tingle with excitement.

Inside the church the people were stirring, gathering their families, heading for their wagons. It did not matter now if someone saw him. He knew what he had to do. He would get his gear and hurry to the Sun Tavern before it was too late.

Chapter 2

Although the rain had stopped long ago, the heavy clouds remained, and an early dusk was settling over the town by the time Jonathan reached the Sun Tavern. Already candles winked from several windows of the tall building that stood behind the Town Hall.

He lingered a moment on the front steps, faintly surprised at the emptiness of the street. Where were all the others who would be hurrying to take up the captain's impassioned challenge? Surely they were already inside.

Gingerly he pushed open the door and stepped in. The room was duskier than the out-of-doors in the ebbing firelight and was practically deserted. A woman carried steaming plates of food to four men knotted around a table in deep conversation. A lone man sat near the door sipping from a tankard. And in the far corner, with his feet propped up on a table, sat Caleb Brewster with his companion.

Brewster's face, which had been ruggedly commanding at the church, was deeply creased, and Jonathan could read the signs of both worry and fatigue in it. The sailor who sat beside him was intent on carving the figure of a mermaid from the foot-long tooth of a sperm whale. Neither man spoke. In the center of the table were a paper, an inkpot, and a quill.

Slowly a tide of fear rose within Jonathan, and he clutched his Brown Bess with sweating hands. Perhaps he had been too hasty. Perhaps he should leave right now.

Suddenly the giant seaman leaped to his feet and slammed his fists on the table. "By heaven, where are they!" he stormed. "They talk about liberty. They shout it in the streets. They cheer at every victory that somebody else wins for 'em. And where are they now that they're needed in this stinking, bloody mess? Trembling! That's where they are. Shaking like wet hounds behind their own locked doors!"

Caleb Brewster sank into his chair as if he had lost the last ounce of strength needed to hold his gigantic frame erect. The four men, who had stopped their conversation to stare, now looked aside in embarrassment, and the lone man put down his tankard and headed for the door.

Jonathan moistened his lips and shouldered his musket. Then he marched up to the table behind which Brewster slouched in a chair and was staring at the floor.

"Sir," he said in a small voice. "I want to enlist."

The burst of laughter that followed Jonathan's announcement nearly swayed him off his feet. The sailor threw back his head, letting go with a giant guffaw. Behind Jonathan the men at the table roared.

Only Caleb Brewster did not laugh. He regarded Jonathan with a sort of puzzled resignation. "I ask for a school of sharks," he said with a sigh, "and the Lord sends me one small minnow."

"I'm not a minnow, sir," said Jonathan, stiffening to his full height. "I'm strong, and I can pull an oar as good as any man. What's more, I'm not afraid."

"Run along, lad," said the sailor, wiping tears of mirth from his eyes with the back of his hand. "You're long on spunk but short on size." Then, turning to Brewster, he added, "From the look on that lad's face, Cale, I'd say ya missed your calling. You shoulda been a preacher like your great-grandpa." With that he broke out in a second fit of laughter.

Brewster scowled at the man and looked at Jonathan thoughtfully. "So you're not afraid, eh?" he said at last. "Do you have a name?"

"Jonathan Barlowe, sir."

"And what of your family? Do they approve of your enlisting?"

"All dead, sir. There's only me." He longed to add, "Free and independent. Answering to no one," but he thought better of it and kept still.

"And how old might you be?"

"Fourteen, sir . . . and a half."

The sailor had gone back to his carving, but he stopped every now and then to chuckle to himself and shake his head. Brewster shifted in his chair and continued to stare at Jonathan, whose heart was pounding so loudly that he was sure the captain could hear it.

"Have you ever shot that thing?" Brewster asked, motioning toward the Brown Bess.

"Sure. Lots of times. And I hit 'em, too," said Jonathan proudly. Then he added with a grin, " 'Course, they mostly were rabbits and quail."

A smile flickered for an instant on Brewster's face and then he said with an air of finality, "In the Continental Artillery a private's pay is $6.67 a month, and you'll serve aboard Mr. Packett here's boat, the *Spindrift*. Read the writing on this paper. That's if you can read. Then put your name under it. That's if you can write."

"What!" shrieked Packett. The whale's tooth hit the table with a thud. "Me wet-nurse a babe on the *Spindrift*? You must of got salt water in your brain!"

"Ned," Brewster said calmly. "I've been thinking it over, and in our special kind of business there's lots of good use to be made of a lad."

Jonathan shuddered. He wasn't sure that he liked the sound of the captain's words, and the old fear, which had subsided only a moment ago, started to grow again.

Packett picked up his whale's tooth and began to carve in silence. Finally he shrugged and said, "Yeah, I guess I see whatcha mean. But mind you, he'll not be coddled."

Jonathan looked wistfully toward the door. He only

wanted to fight for his country's independence. He did not want to get involved in any special business. If he ducked out now, before he signed the enlistment paper, maybe he would not have to.

"I thought you weren't afraid," boomed the captain as if he had read Jonathan's thoughts.

Jonathan swallowed hard and picked up the quill and dipped it into the inkpot. It was too late. "No, sir," he muttered as he scrawled his name across the page. Then, squinting in the dim firelight, he read the terms of his enlistment.

> We whose names are under written, do hereby enlist ourselves as soldiers in the American continental army, for one year, unless sooner discharged, and do furnish ourselves each with a good effective fire arm and blanket, and if possible, a bayonet, a cartridge box, or in lieu of a bayonet, a hatchet or tomahawk. And we do bind ourselves to conform in all instances to such rules and regulations, as are, or shall be, established for the government of said army.
>
> June 4, 1779

Jonathan placed the quill on the table and stood at attention facing the captain.

"Lieutenant Packett whaled with me in the North Atlantic, and he knows what he's about," said Brewster. "Never forget that, and never fail to obey his orders the same as if they were mine. We leave from Penfield's tide mill tonight at midnight. Be there!" Dismissing Jonathan with a wave of his hand, Brewster turned to Packett, and the two men began talking in low tones.

Jonathan walked briskly as he left the Sun Tavern, his misgivings of a few minutes ago forgotten. Midnight. The tiny boats would slip across Long Island Sound under the cover of darkness to raid the sleeping enemy on the other side. His heart pounded in anticipation.

There were still a few coins left from the sale of the wagon and team so that Jonathan could easily have taken his supper at the Sun Tavern, but he was too excited to be hungry. Instead he pulled a hunk of coarse, brown bread out of his knapsack and turned down Beach Road toward the shore. He had taken the bread along when he left the Gladdens' house this morning in the pouring rain to pay his final respects to his father before setting out on his own. So much had happened since then that it seemed more than a day away.

Midnight was still a long while off when Jonathan reached the beach. The wind was still, and the moon and stars were hidden by a low-slung canopy of clouds. The only sound was the soft whisper of waves breaking over the sand. He shivered as he looked out across the black water and remembered Captain Brewster's fiery warning that the men who signed with him would learn firsthand why Long Island Sound was called the Devil's Belt.

Jonathan turned east toward Penfield's tide mill and scuffed along the high-tide line. Shells, seaweed, driftwood, and other oddments abandoned in the scuttle of the last receding tide made walking difficult, so he moved down to the smooth-swept sand at the water's edge. He sauntered along, stopping now and then to turn and watch the waves make tiny tide pools of the row of footprints that he left behind.

The end of the storm had brought chilly air, and the moisture on the warm sand began to form a thin mist that rose and swirled eerily about him. Jonathan tried to shrug away a closed-in feeling as he remembered the time he had first seen fog as a small boy. For a moment he had thought that it was snow, higher than the trees, but then he had known that it was not. Slowly he had been seized with the awful notion that the world he loved and longed for had been magically erased by this silent, creeping whiteness. All the pulsing color and vibrant sounds had been reduced to the prison of a tailor's wagon. He had been afraid to go to sleep that night for fear that when he awoke the next day he would find that the world truly was gone. But by the time he opened his eyes the morning sun had burned away all but a few trailing wisps. Nevertheless, the old fear haunted him each time the fog spread its ghostly shroud.

Jonathan squinted in the darkness. It was difficult to see far ahead. Still, he knew that there was little to see, just inky water to the right and gray beach fringed with tall grass and scrub pine to the left. Slowly a long, low object, half in the water and half out, took form directly ahead. Driftwood, he mused. He could stop there for a bit. He still had plenty of time. But the presence of the fog urged him to quicken his step. He needed the reassuring sight of Black Rock Harbor.

A few feet from the driftwood Jonathan stopped short. It was not driftwood at all. It was a man, face down, splayed like a starfish in the sand.

Jonathan gasped. His first instinct was to run, but he forced himself to stay. He stood there for a long time staring down before he dropped to his knees beside the still figure.

The man, who was short and stockily built, was icy cold to the touch, and his shirt and breeches clung to him like frost. Jonathan slipped his hands under the man's thick chest and rolled him onto his back. His head lolled to one side, and his eyes fixed Jonathan with a ghostly stare. Trembling, Jonathan lifted the man's wrist. His dangling hand swayed slightly as Jonathan tried to find a pulse. No luck. Jonathan's heart began to pound, and he dropped the arm as if it were a snake. Surely he could not be dead.

Shakily, Jonathan bent low and placed an ear on the man's chest. Nothing. He pressed closer, hoping for the slightest trace, until his ear was numb from the cold.

Out of the corner of his eye on the upturned side of his face, Jonathan saw something move. He raised his head in time to see a dark figure just as a jarring smash on the back of his head made lights flash in his brain. Then everything went black.

Chapter 3

The first thing Jonathan saw when he opened his eyes was the cheery blaze of a campfire. He raised himself up on an elbow, rubbing first his eyes and then the walnut-sized knot that throbbed on the back of his head.

"Sorry about that."

Jonathan caught his breath as the blurry figure of a man seemed to rise above the fire like smoke. Jonathan rubbed his eyes again and saw to his great relief that the smiling man who addressed him was standing on the other side of the fire rather than hovering above it.

"I thought you were robbing old Zeke, and Lord knows he's had enough trouble for one day without robbers."

The man came around the fire and knelt beside Jonathan. "Name's Bracy Gwinnett," he said, still smiling. "Me and Zeke were fishermen. Didn't have a regular port. Just caught and sold 'em wherever we pleased. We were out on the Sound last night when the storm broke and our boat turned turtle, spilling us and all we had into the drink. I've been combing the beach since dawn lookin' for him. Then I came across you bending over his corpse, and I guess you can figure out the rest."

Jonathan nodded and smiled back at the tall, dark-haired young man, whom he judged to be not over twenty. His face was handsome, but it seemed pale in the glow of the fire, and his ill-fitting clothes hung loose, as if some sickness had made him thin.

"I'm Jonathan Barlowe . . . of the Continental Artillery," he said with pride, and he noted a flicker in Gwinnett's eyes.

"Aren't you a bit young to be in the army?"

"Oh, I'm involved in special business with Captain Caleb Brewster," said Jonathan. "We're leaving at midnight for Long Island and a special mission he's got cooked up. He's lookin' for recruits, if you'd care to come along."

Gwinnett became lost in thought, and the smile almost faded from his face, but it bobbed back an instant later as he said, "Caleb Brewster, eh? Yes. I've heard of him. Just might give your offer some thought, since I've lost my boat, which was all I had in the world, and my partner, too. Buried him while you were sleepin'."

"Sleeping! You mean I slept *that* long?" cried Jonathan. He jumped to his feet, but was pushed down again by the dizzying pain at the back of his head.

"Take it easy," said Gwinnett with a chuckle. "It'll

be a while before you can move very fast. I gave you a pretty stiff whack."

"You don't understand," Jonathan insisted. "The boats leave Penfield's tide mill at midnight, and I have to be there."

Gwinnett reached out a hand and helped Jonathan to his feet. "Well, then, Jonny my friend," he said cheerily. "We'll just have to see to it that you get there."

Jonathan stood aside, gathering his strength while Gwinnett covered the fire with sand and picked up the knapsack and musket. Then, using his new friend as a crutch, Jonathan hurried in the direction of the tide mill as fast as his shaky legs would carry him and prayed that he would not be too late.

Most of the fog had dissipated now. As they neared the warehouse-lined harbor the kelpy smell of the sea was strong, and once in a while the breeze brought a stunning whiff from fishing boats cradled in their moorings for the night. A skinny dog sniffed around a stack of lobster pots, but nothing else stirred on the deserted pier.

Jonathan hardly dared breathe. "What if they've gone?" he whispered hoarsely.

"Well, I expect then you'll have to go off somewhere and find yourself a new line of work if you don't want to be shot as a deserter," Gwinnett said with a laugh. "But wait," he added. "Aren't those your whaleboats up yonder?"

Forgetting the ache in his head, Jonathan pulled away

27

from his companion and clattered up the wooden wharf to where six longboats bobbed in the water like a school of bluefish. On the bow of the third boat was the word *Spindrift*.

"Bracy, it's here! It's here!" cried Jonathan, jumping up and down. "We're in time after all."

Jonathan stared at the boat in awe. It looked to be nearly thirty feet long, pointed at both bow and stern. An enormous swivel gun was mounted menacingly on the port side near the bow.

Gwinnett gave out a low whistle of admiration as he stepped alongside Jonathan. "Ain't she a beaut?"

"Bracy, you've got to come with us. Say you will."

Gwinnett smiled and clamped one hand on Jonathan's shoulder in fatherly fashion. He looked out across the dark water. "All right," he said at last. "Why not? Let's find your Captain Brewster so I can sign on."

Past the pier and straddling the banks on the western shore of Black Rock Harbor stood Penfield's tide mill, creaking softly as water sluiced through its wheel. Jonathan paused at the door of the old millhouse and took a deep breath of the sweet night air. As soon as he walked through that door he would be a soldier and nothing would ever be the same again.

"Ready?" he whispered into the darkness.

"Ready," was Gwinnett's steady reply.

Jonathan lifted the latch and shoved open the heavy door. Inside were a dozen or so men, some sitting on the dirt floor of the large empty room, some standing, a few talking. A ship's lantern in one corner cast a soft light over the knapsacks and muskets that littered the floor. Caleb Brewster stood alone, and he was so deep in thought that he did not appear to notice when Jonathan and his new friend came in.

"Captain Brewster, sir?" Bracy Gwinnett's voice cut into Jonathan's thoughts, and he watched Gwinnett stride up to the huge seaman with a casualness that he could not help but admire.

Brewster's clouded eyes were alert at once. He acknowledged Gwinnett's presence with a sharp nod.

"I understand from one of your men that you're needing recruits, and I've come to see about signing on."

Brewster shot a quick glance at Jonathan and then slowly looked Gwinnett up and down.

Leaving Gwinnett to complete his business with Brewster, Jonathan turned away and looked around the room. Counting himself and Gwinnett, there were still only seventeen men, certainly not a large-enough force for a battle. Perhaps Brewster had arranged to meet other boats across the Sound, he thought. That must be it. There certainly would not be much that they could do alone.

He bounced his musket nervously in his hands and waited. None of the crew had so much as looked his way. They were an odd-looking bunch, he thought. Most wore some grimy combination of the uniform of the artilleryman and the seaman's garb, but they all had sea-tanned faces and calloused hands, and Jonathan wondered how long it would take them to accept him as one of the crew.

"It's time," barked the captain so sharply that Jonathan nearly dropped his musket. "We're taking only the *Spindrift* tonight."

Slowly the crewmen picked up their belongings and queued up in front of Brewster. Packett was first in line.

"What are they doing that for?" Jonathan whispered to Gwinnett, who had come to stand beside him. Bracy shrugged and took his place with the others. Jonathan followed, standing at the end of the line.

Brewster reached into a knapsack beside him on the floor and drew out a bottle. He pulled the cork with his teeth, spat it into the dirt, and raised the bottle over his head. "To our mission . . . and to our new recruits, Barlowe and Gwinnett." With that he threw back his head and swigged deeply from the bottle. With a satisfied sigh he passed the bottle on to Packett.

The crew nodded and each man murmured an echo of the captain's toast as he took his turn at the bottle. "West India Rum" the label read, and Jonathan watched it come closer and closer, hoping that it would be empty by the time it got to him. Each man broke from the line after he had had his turn and followed the bottle along as it passed from hand to hand.

Finally only Bracy and Jonathan were left, standing within the circle of men. Bracy swallowed his portion without so much as a flinch and passed the bottle to Jonathan.

"Just a tot now, lad," cautioned Packett, and some of the others chuckled.

Jonathan stared at the bottle in his hand as if it were a British soldier. He would have to drink it, he told himself sternly. Otherwise he would never be accepted. They would think he was a babe. Slowly he raised the bottle to his lips, trying not to see the amused looks on the faces all around him. Suddenly the rum touched his mouth and raced like wildfire down his tongue and into his throat. Jonathan gasped, dropping the bottle. Tears flooded his eyes. It felt as if his entire throat were being clawed away.

"Swallow!" someone shouted, and slapped him on the back.

Jonathan swallowed and gasped again, fighting with all his might to hold back the cough that was bursting to get out.

A cheer went up from the crew and more hands slapped him on the back. Jonathan tried to smile as he followed the men out of the mill. He was one of them now.

The crewmen filed into the *Spindrift* and pulled the oars out from under the plank seats, stowing their gear where the oars had been. Jonathan and Bracy followed, doing whatever the others did. They found seats exactly opposite one another, Gwinnett to port and Jonathan to starboard, just three spaces up from the stern, where Packett stood by the tiller. In the bow Caleb Brewster leaned against the side, one hand resting on the swivel gun.

"How's your head?" asked Gwinnett as the mate prepared to cast off.

"All right," said Jonathan, who had forgotten all about the painful knot in the excitement of his first army mission. As if mentioning it had triggered it again, the low throb started up in the back of his head and kept time with the pull of the oars.

Soon they were headed for open water, leaving behind the deserted harbor and gliding past the glimmering lights of Black Rock Fort. The swollen clouds of a few hours before had thinned to wispy tatters, and a breeze freshened from the west, gently scalloping the surface of the Sound.

Jonathan was tired from the long day, and his untrained arms soon began to ache from rowing. Still, his spirits were high, and he closed his eyes as he rowed, thinking that there was no place in the world where he would rather be.

Suddenly there was a commotion in the bow of the boat. Jonathan opened his eyes in time to see the captain swing around and shout to the crew, "Halt your rowing! British frigate dead ahead!"

Chapter 4

Jonathan squinted around the heads of the sailors in front of him. Sure enough, a black shape was moving out of a blacker background, masts silhouetted against the sky. On a signal from the captain, the sailors stilled the thudding oars and sat tensely in their seats. An eerie melody of creaks and groans floated in the air as the wind played the rigging of the menacing ship like harp strings.

The vessel was moving west across the *Spindrift*'s path, and it grew larger as it came closer. It's tacking, Jonathan thought, zigzagging to catch the wind in her sails. It can't come much closer without seeing us.

He counted thirty gunports, all open, with guns ready to fire on the tiny rowboat at a moment's notice. Brewster slowly turned the solitary swivel gun toward the ship and bent low to sight it.

Jonathan caught his breath. Was the man mad? Surely he would not fire on·a British warship.

He swallowed hard, and the sound echoed in his ears like a crashing wave. All around him the men sat frozen, their eyes on the approaching ship.

A picture leaped into Jonathan's mind of a barrage of fire from the massive bank of guns and the whaleboat splintering in the air. He could almost feel the icy water of the Devil's Belt closing over his head as he struggled to find something to cling to. Instead the graceful frigate suddenly turned in her tacking maneuver and glided away into the night. The sigh from the crew came almost in unison.

Brewster waited until the ship had completely disappeared from sight before giving the signal to row. Jonathan gripped his oar and found to his surprise that his hands were trembling. He glanced at Bracy with a half-embarrassed grin, but his friend was looking toward the spot where the frigate had disappeared. The strangely quizzical smile on Gwinnett's face sent an unexpected shiver through Jonathan, and he turned back to his rowing without a word.

They had lost precious time sitting dead in the water and had drifted slightly off course with the tide, so it was almost dawn before the *Spindrift* rounded Old Field Point on Long Island. They dragged the boat through the reedy marshes that dotted the narrow sandspit at Setauket beach and soon were rowing across Conscience Bay, their oars leaving a herringbone wake in the calm water. Suddenly the sun burst over the rolling hills, turning the bay into a pool of gold. In the bow Brewster leaned against the swivel gun and moved it slowly from one side to another as he carefully scanned the shoreline. All was quiet. He signaled to Packett, who skillfully guided the boat into one of the clumps of willows that fringed the bay. There, where waterbugs skimmed the water and dragonflies droned in the still air, they were completely out of sight from both water and land.

Jonathan was still puzzled. He had seen no enemy garrisons on the hillsides, no other whaleboats in the bay. What was this strange mission that they were on?

He did not have long to wonder. "Barlowe, you come with Packett and me," shouted the captain. "The rest of you men stay on board. Keep quiet and out of sight."

Jonathan stood up on unsteady legs, remembering Brewster's words of last night, "In our special kind of business there's lots of good use to be made of a lad." His pulse began to race. What were they going to do with him? Use him as some kind of bait? He looked quickly at Bracy, who only tipped an imaginary hat and smiled at him, but not before Jonathan had seen a trace of irritation on his face.

Brewster led them away from the boat to a place well out of earshot. Then, turning to Jonathan, he said, "Lad, I have an errand for you. It won't be hard and it shouldn't take you long, but it is important. Over that hill is a road. It leads into the town of Setauket. Go to the Roe Tavern and ask to speak to Austin Roe. Talk to no one along the way and to him only when there's no one else about. Tell him that you've come to pick up a package for John Bolton. When you have the package, come straight back here. Think you've got that?"

"Yes, sir. I'm to go to the Roe Tavern, speak to Austin Roe, and ask for a package for John Bolton. Is . . . is that all, sir?"

"That's it," said Brewster with a sigh. "And good luck." Packett nodded and murmured the same.

Jonathan bounded over the hill and lit out down the road with a strut. I, Jonathan Barlowe of the Continental Army, am off on a secret mission in enemy territory, he thought, and could not suppress a grin. Maybe Austin Roe is really a spy and maybe this mysterious package is full of documents stolen from a British general. Humming a tune, Jonathan stuck out his chest and marched importantly toward Setauket.

At the beginning of his journey the road had been deserted and the farms spread far apart, but as he neared town, signs of life were everywhere. An elegant lady in a covered chaise waved to him as she passed, and a wagging collie dog ran to greet him from beside a farmhouse door. Farmers plowed their fields, and smoke drifted lazily from chimneys.

This sure doesn't look like enemy territory, he thought. It just looks like any old ordinary place.

He heard the sound of approaching horses. They were coming from behind at a fast clip, and he spun around to see two British soldiers bearing down on him.

Jonathan stopped dead still. There was no doubt now that this was enemy territory. If only he had his musket. What if they stopped him and asked where he was going? What would he say? Of course he did not have on a uniform. Perhaps if he did nothing to arouse their suspicion they would pass on by. He tried to strike a sauntering gait, easy and natural, but his feet and legs seemed to belong to someone else, and a couple of times he almost stumbled. He puckered up his lips to whistle, but all that came out was a hiss.

The soldiers were close now. He could smell the dust churned into the air by crashing hooves. A moment later they thundered by without hesitation.

His lungs bursting, Jonathan stopped and exhaled. He realized in surprise that it was the first time he had breathed since he heard the soldiers coming up behind him. He watched them disappear down the road. Their coats were a brilliant red and their sabers glinted in the morning sunlight.

Jonathan shivered. Perhaps his mission was more dangerous than he had thought. Still, he had fooled those British soldiers into thinking that he was just an ordinary civilian. Perhaps in Setauket they would think that, too. Nevertheless, his uneasiness increased when he entered the streets of the town. The red-coated soldiers were everywhere, cantering up and down the streets, lounging on porches. There was a tenseness in the air, and the people hurried about their business, scarcely looking up to greet each other.

To Jonathan's great relief, no one paid the slightest bit of attention to him as he went toward the heart of town, where he was sure he would find the Roe Tavern.

He charted his course by heading for a towering church spire that pointed toward heaven, but he caught his breath when he rounded the last corner and stood before the church in the village green.

A sign on the front proclaimed it to be the Presbyterian church, but instead it looked like a fortress. The church and a stockade made of gravestones that had been ripped from the cemetery were surrounded by heavy breastworks, and the ugly snouts of swivel guns poked through the fragments of once beautiful stained-glass windows.

A pair of British soldiers stood on the front steps, laughing together at some private joke, and Jonathan knew that he should not linger there in full view of the enemy. He tried to move away, but the sight of the violated church and its cemetery brought to mind the quiet Connecticut churchyard where his father had been laid to rest. This kind of thing must never happen there. He was a soldier. He would not let it.

Jonathan found the Roe Tavern several blocks away, and when he entered he was greeted by the smell of whale-oil lamps and ale mingled with the aroma of fresh-baked bread. In his excitement he had forgotten how long it had been since he had eaten, and now, deep inside, his stomach began to rumble. A few minutes later a pretty young woman in a starched white mob cap and apron served him a heaping plate of cold beef and hot bread and a fat mug of buttermilk.

When he had finished eating he sat back and looked around the crowded room trying to decide which of the men was Austin Roe, the one he was looking for. He would certainly not be one of the several British soldiers intent on their midday meal, but which of the others he might be Jonathan could not decide, so when the young woman returned to clear away his plate and mug, he asked importantly, "Where might I find a gentleman named Austin Roe? I have business which must be conducted in private."

"I'll send him to you," she said softly, barely looking up.

A moment later a thin, hawk-faced man slid into the barrel-back chair beside Jonathan. "I'm Austin Roe," he drawled pleasantly. "You say you have business with me?"

"Yes. I . . . uh," Jonathan stammered. "I've come to pick up a package for John Bolton."

A flash of surprise showed in Austin Roe's eyes, but then he smiled and said, "Why, certainly. I'll have it for you right away."

Jonathan felt pleased as the man left the table and he looked smugly at a red-coated soldier who was heading for the door. Austin Roe was scarcely gone when he returned again, and Jonathan saw with a stab of disappointment that the important package was nothing more than a long loaf of bread.

"Here you are, my boy," said Roe, handing the bread to Jonathan. "Hot from the oven, just the way Mr. Bolton likes it."

Jonathan took the bread and murmured "Thank you" without looking up. He did not want the man to see the embarrassment that must surely show on his face.

Outside the tavern door Jonathan broke into a run, and he did not slow down until he had reached the quiet countryside beyond the town. He had never been so humiliated. He could imagine how Brewster and Packett must have laughed, telling him that he was a soldier off on a special mission and then sending him to fetch a loaf of bread while they went into battle.

Who was John Bolton, anyway? He didn't know any John Bolton. It was probably just a name that Brewster had made up. Maybe Brewster thought the same as Packett, that he was a babe. Maybe they had let him come along just to help with the rowing, and now they were sending him away before the fighting started.

Jonathan bristled at the thought and picked up a rock and hurled it as hard as he could against a tree. Some war for freedom this was, walking into town in broad daylight without even so much as a musket and picking up a loaf of bread. If that was the kind of orders his captain gave, perhaps he should not go back. Perhaps he should do what he had intended to do in the first place, go off on his own, free and independent, answering to no one. At least he would have a loaf of bread to eat. If only he had brought his knapsack and Brown Bess.

Jonathan scuffed along the road, still heading toward the bay and the waiting whaleboat. He was tired from a full night of rowing, and the meadow grass beside the road looked soft and inviting. Nevertheless, he knew that a good soldier always followed orders. Perhaps

Brewster had been testing him and had given him this order to see if a boy of only fourteen could be counted on to do his duty. He would have to find out before he took a chance on being shot for a deserter.

Jonathan topped the last hill and saw the waters of Conscience Bay winking up at him in the afternoon sunshine, but Caleb Brewster was nowhere to be seen. Perhaps he had taken the whaleboat, after all, and left Jonathan in enemy territory with only a loaf of bread. Breaking into a run, he careened down the hillside toward the willow-lined bank.

"Barlowe! Over here."

Jonathan whirled around quickly toward the place from where the voice had come and saw Brewster's shaggy head protruding from a ferny clump of willows. He was filled with a mixture of relief and dread. At least he had not been abandoned, but how could he face the captain? What would he say?

Brewster did not give him time for words. He stepped outside the tent of trees and grabbed the loaf of bread the moment Jonathan came near. "Get in the boat," he ordered.

Jonathan parted the curtain of leaves and climbed slowly into the long whaleboat, but the captain did not follow. The other oarsmen, who milled around in the stern of the boat, eyed him curiously as he headed for his place, and he could feel a blush spreading over his face.

They know, he thought bitterly. They know, and inside they're probably laughing.

"Where've you been, Jonny my friend?" Bracy Gwinnett asked brightly.

Without meaning to, Jonathan looked up. "Oh, nowhere much," he said with an embarrassed shrug. "Just on an errand for the captain."

"Well, he probably thought you were a bit too young to go out scouting the enemy with the rest of us. Could have been dangerous, you know."

"Well, I'm not too young," cried Jonathan. "I'm a private in the Continental Artillery and as good a soldier as any man. And what's more, I'm tired of being treated like a babe!"

Jonathan could feel all eyes upon him as he stood in the center of the boat trembling with rage. Gwinnett looked startled and fumbled for words, but before he could answer, Brewster appeared. He no longer had the loaf of bread.

As Brewster jumped into the boat and gave the order to cast off, Jonathan sat down quickly. He felt that at any moment he was going to be sick.

Chapter 5

A gimpy little man wearing the black knit hat of a
sailor was fidgeting nervously beside the empty moor-
ing when the *Spindrift* pulled into Black Rock Harbor
four hours later. Jonathan did not recognize the man,
but Brewster obviously knew him, because he sprang
out of the boat as soon as it bumped against the pilings
and the two stepped into the shadows, where they
spoke together in low tones.

A sailor leaped ashore and caught the hawser as
Packett barked orders from the stern. When the boat
had been secured he called out, "Be at Penfield's tide
mill at midnight tomorrow night." Then he leaned
back against the tiller and watched the crew gather their
belongings and file onto the wharf to disappear into the
night.

"Barlowe," shouted the captain.

"Yes, sir," he answered, leaping onto the wooden
planking that formed the wharf. Maybe he had proved
himself to the captain after all. Maybe now he was
going to be sent on an important mission.

"There's a horse tied at Penfield's tide mill," said Brewster, stepping out of the shadows.

"Yes?" Jonathan's pulse quickened.

"Bring it to me on the double."

Jonathan jerked around and hurried toward the tide mill. Fetch a loaf of bread. Fetch a horse. Next time he'll probably throw sticks for me to fetch, he thought. A horse whinnied softly in the darkness ahead and Jonathan stumbled toward it, fighting to hold back tears. It was crazy to enlist, he thought. I'm not on my own. I'm no better off than before. All I did was trade a tailor's wagon for a whaleboat.

A prancing stallion glistened in the moonlight. Jonathan forgot his anger as his hand closed around the rein, which was tied to a post beside the front door to the mill.

"Whoa there. Whoa, boy," he whispered, and gently stroked the animal's soft neck. When the horse was calm he sprang into the saddle. The stirrups hung several inches below his feet, but that did not diminish the grand feeling that surged through him. With a horse like this he could ride like the wind, chase the enemy, thunder into battle.

Jonathan had learned how to ride during the past summer, when his father had worked for a rich farmer. It took him several weeks to stitch up all the clothes the farmer's large family needed, and during that time Jonathan had become good friends with the eldest son, a boy his own age. The two had spent every free afternoon riding together. Jonathan had never been happier, and ever since then he had secretly dreamed of having a horse of his own.

Jonathan looked longingly at the dark countryside to the north. There were plenty of places to hide in the thickly wooded hills of Connecticut. But then he would be a deserter as well as a horse thief. Besides, the captain had said to bring the horse on the double and he had lingered long enough.

The stranger was gone by the time Jonathan returned to the dock. Everyone else was gone, too, except for Bracy, who lolled against a post, and Brewster, who paced back and forth impatiently in front of the *Spindrift*. He grunted a thank you and mounted the horse as soon as Jonathan slid to the ground. Wheeling, he headed his mount toward the north and thundered out of sight in the darkness.

"Looks like we're on our own," said Bracy as he sauntered toward Jonathan. "Packett said that most of the crew live right here in Fairfield, so there's no place to billet us when we're not on a mission. But I know a spot with a great view of the water. Of course it's pretty sandy and awfully damp when it rains. Tomorrow we'll have to look for better quarters."

Jonathan stiffened. The last thing he wanted was to be treated like a little brother. If only he could be on his own for a few hours away from everyone until he could get over his humiliation. All during the trip home across the Sound he had kept a sharp look out for a British craft. If they could just get into a battle, he had thought, not with a huge warship like the frigate they had seen on the way over, but with a small vessel that they could handle, then perhaps he could prove to the captain how good a soldier he really was.

But they had not sighted a ship of any size. They had not even seen one of the Tory whaleboats, which, like Brewster's fleet of rowboats, moved back and forth across the Devil's Belt like giant centipedes.

At the beginning of the war, so he had been told, the shores of Long Island Sound had been littered with abandoned and rotting whaleboats that were the relics of a once great industry when the small inland sea abounded in whales. By the start of the Revolutionary War the whaling industry had all but died out, but the long rowboats had been ideally suited to the type of raiding and plundering that went on constantly between the Whigs in Connecticut and the Tories on Long Island, not to mention the warring armies, and they had been quickly refurbished and outfitted for battle.

Jonathan had still been filled with disappointment when they reached the Connecticut shore, and now he stared at the buckles on his shoes, feeling more dejected than ever.

Bracy draped a long, thin arm around his shoulders. "That Brewster's a real rat for treating you the way he did," he said with a sigh. "Where did he send you today, anyway?"

"To fetch a loaf of bread," Jonathan growled. It was good to be able to talk about it, and he gathered his gear and followed Bracy down the beach, pouring out the whole miserable story.

They walked along in silence after Jonathan had finished talking. Bracy seemed to be lost in thought. Finally he stopped. "Jonny my friend," he said. "*I* have a mission for you, and it's not to fetch a loaf of bread."

Jonathan swallowed hard and stared at Gwinnett in disbelief. "You have a mission for me?" he whispered.

"Yes. A very important mission, and if it works the way I think it will, you're going to be a hero."

Without another word Bracy dropped his gear in the sand and began gathering pieces of driftwood and dry seaweed and arranging them in a pile. Jonathan watched nervously. Bracy had said that he could be a hero. Why didn't he tell him more?

With maddening slowness, Bracy drew a flint and steel out of his pack and struck them together once, twice. Finally, on the third try, they sparked and a brilliant flame flared against the blackness.

At last Bracy turned toward Jonathan, and there was a rapturous glow on his face as he spoke again. "I have a cousin who lives in Setauket. He only pretends to be loyal to the British crown, because he doesn't want to leave his home and livelihood, but he's as dedicated to throwing off the yoke of tyranny as you and I." Bracy paused and put a hand on Jonathan's shoulder. When he spoke he was looking Jonathan straight in the eye, and his slow, deliberate words had a deadly seriousness about them that sent a shiver up Jonathan's spine.

"If you can get a message to him the next time the captain sends you on some silly errand, maybe we can work out a way for him to keep us informed on what the British are doing in Setauket."

Bracy paused again, giving his words time to sink in, and Jonathan shook his head. It was a preposterous idea. A spy operation—that was what Bracy was suggesting. He actually wanted Jonathan to set up a spy operation. A lump of cold fear sank to the pit of his stomach.

"Wouldn't it be dangerous?" he asked weakly.

"So's being a soldier," said Bracy, jabbing the flaming logs with a long piece of driftwood. "Look at it this way: it would make things a lot safer for all of us if the captain knew exactly where the enemy was and what they were up to. Besides, when he finds out about your part in it, he'll have to see that you're more than just an errand boy."

Jonathan knew that what Bracy was saying was true. He would never get another chance like this one, and he stared into the fire and tried to imagine the look on Brewster's face when he marched up to him and handed him a map or a letter full of intelligence information.

"We'd better get some sleep now," said Bracy abruptly, bringing Jonathan back to reality. "We can finish working out our plans in the morning."

Jonathan nodded his agreement and stretched out in

the sand, using his knapsack for a pillow. Soon Bracy was snoring loudly, but Jonathan was too excited to fall asleep. He lay awake for a long time, staring at the ceiling of stars and thinking about his new mission.

This time tomorrow night I might be on my way to being a spy, he thought. He turned on his side and fell asleep, dreaming.

Chapter 6

The next morning Jonathan and Bracy went into Fairfield to find a place to stay and to get some supplies. Bracy had lost everything except the clothes he was wearing when his boat capsized in Long Island Sound, but Jonathan still had a few coins from the sale of his father's wagon and team, and they started the day with a hearty breakfast at the Sun Tavern. The innkeeper at the tavern told them about an elderly widow named Mrs. Hoad who kept a boarding house on the Post Road. A couple of Brewster's unmarried crewmen lived there, he said.

After breakfast they went to see her. Mrs. Hoad was prune-faced and sharp-eyed, but her smile was kindly enough. She showed them a spacious corner room and told them they could share it for three dollars a month apiece.

It was a comfortable room, clean swept, and furnished with two feather beds, a washstand, and a writing table and chair. Jonathan looked longingly at one of the feather beds while Mrs. Hoad explained the boardinghouse rules. The moment she left the room he jumped into the center of the downy mattress and snuggled into its delicious softness.

Settling in made the rest of the day pass quickly. Then, at midnight sharp, the *Spindrift* cast off from Black Rock Harbor under a moon the shape of a cat's claw. Jonathan rowed in jerky strokes, finding it hard to keep rhythm with the others in his excitement. He and Bracy had spent the afternoon making their plans, and now a letter to Bracy's cousin, Levi Adams, lay hidden under his shirt. It felt as big as a boulder. He wished Bracy had let him read it before he sealed it with the brownish sealing wax, but he had told Jonathan what it said and that was really all that mattered.

Jonathan worried most about Bracy's cousin. "He has strange ways and he's a bit of a ruffian," Bracy had said, "but he won't hurt you. Especially once he knows you've been sent by me." The warning had come with Bracy's usual ear-to-ear grin, so that Jonathan was not certain just how serious he had been. All the same, the thought was not very comforting, and he tried to push the image out of his mind as they moved swiftly across the Devil's Belt.

The sky was filled with the soft gray glow that precedes dawn when they pulled into the willows on the far side of Conscience Bay. Jonathan stowed his oar and waited tensely. What if Brewster did not send him on another errand? He would lose his chance to be a spy and the captain might think of him as a babe forever.

Packett handed out meager rations, which consisted

of cold biscuits and dried beef. They could not risk a fire to boil coffee, and they choked down the hard, dry food in silence. Brewster paced back and forth in the narrow bow of the boat watching the sun rise slowly in the sky. Finally he motioned Jonathan to him.

"I have an order here for some goods that we can't get in Connecticut because the supply lines have been cut off by the British," Brewster said. He reached down into a pouch at his feet and brought out a letter sealed with a glob of blue wax. He handed it to Jonathan. "Take this order to Austin Roe, and he'll see that it's filled by the next time we come to Setauket."

Jonathan nodded solemnly, took the letter, and stuffed it inside his shirt with the letter for Levi Adams.

"Remember," Brewster cautioned. "Conduct your business with no one but Austin Roe himself."

Jonathan's feelings were mixed as he hurried up the hill that led to Old Field Road and Setauket. On the one hand, he was glad to have an errand to do that would give him a chance to complete his spy mission, but on the other, he could see that Brewster had not changed his opinion of him. He supposed that he knew now what Brewster had meant when he said to Packett that there was lots of good use to be made of a lad. He had meant that he would not have to take a real soldier away from the battles if there was a boy around to do the chores.

Well, all of that will change before long, he thought, and chuckled to himself.

Bracy had said that he would come to the road to Levi Adams' house about a mile before he reached the outskirts of Setauket. Jonathan decided to see Adams first and conduct his important business before he delivered the order to Austin Roe, which most likely was for nothing more than shoe buckles and lace.

The crossroad was just as Bracy had described it. An outcropping of rock and a tall stand of beech trees partially concealed a fieldstone farmhouse with a windmill spinning in the front yard. He turned into the road, and then, a few yards past the farmhouse, turned left again into a narrow lane that should lead him to the home of Levi Adams.

Jonathan's pulse quickened as he jogged along. What if Mr. Adams was not at home? Or what if he was and he was really the ruffian that Bracy had said?

To Jonathan's surprise, the lane ended at a ramshackle cabin. A pair of bowlegged posts held up a frowning front-porch roof. The shutters drooped and the chimney had lost several large stones.

He remembered what Bracy had said about his cousin's not wanting to leave his home or his livelihood. That seemed pretty strange if this place was his home, and there certainly were no visible signs that he had any kind of livelihood. But then Bracy had also said that Levi Adams had strange ways.

Tiptoeing up onto the creaking front porch, Jonathan tapped timidly on the front door. He waited a moment and then pressed his ear against the boards.

There was no sound inside. He knocked again, rapping harder this time. Still, no one answered the door.

He should have gone to the Roe Tavern first, anyway, he reasoned. After all, he was a soldier in the Continental Army and he was under orders to deliver a letter. He would come back here again after he had seen Austin Roe.

As he started to leave he heard a low rumble, punctuated by a slow hoofbeat. Jonathan turned toward the weary sound and, to his great surprise, saw a patched and dingy sail rising above the undergrowth just past the bend in the road. It seemed to be floating slowly toward the cabin.

"What!" he gasped. "A boat pulled by a horse?"

Jonathan stood unblinking on the sagging porch for what seemed like an hour. Finally around the bend came a goat, its head drooping. Behind it bounced a rickety cart with a small sail puffing breathlessly in and out in the uncertain breeze. There was no driver on the front seat of the cart, but the goat seemed to know where it was going and he pulled up to a stop beside the porch.

The goat eyed Jonathan warily but made no sound. Jonathan eyed him back and made a wide path around it to peer over the side of the cart. The body of a man lay sprawled face down in the bottom.

Jonathan swallowed hard. Another corpse! He tried to run, but a hand shot out of the cart and grabbed his arm and a voice boomed in his ear. "Aha! I've caught you now, haven't I?"

Slowly Jonathan turned his head until he faced the man who had been lying in the bottom of the cart only a few seconds ago. He was very much alive and he reeked of rum. His eyes were bloodshot and bleary, and his nose was bulbous and crisscrossed with purple veins.

"I can't go into town for a tot of rum without you hooligans stealin' me blind. Well, I've caught you this time, I have."

"I'm not a thief," Jonathan sputtered. "I'm a friend of Bracy Gwinnett. And if you be Levi Adams, I've a letter for you."

"Are you and Bracy Gwinnett in the same kettle of soup? Now that's about as odd as huckleberry chowder."

Releasing Jonathan's arm, the man stumbled out of the cart and up to the door of the cabin, but the goat did not take its eyes off Jonathan. "Of course I'm Levi Adams," the man called over his shoulder. "Come on in and show me this letter you say you've got."

Jonathan nervously made another wide arc around the glaring goat and followed Adams into the cabin. The man was a ruffian, all right. Maybe he should try again to run. But it was too late. The door slammed shut behind him.

The room was a jumble. Dirty clothes littered the floor and half-eaten food rotted on the table. Adams kicked aside an overturned chair as he strode to the fireplace and leaned against it. He took a hunting knife from among the clutter on the mantel and scratched the stubble on his chin with its point. Raising one eyebrow, he looked sternly at Jonathan.

"Well, where is it?" he demanded.

Jonathan reached a trembling hand inside his shirt and drew out the letter. Adams' hand swooped through the air like a diving gull and grabbed it before Jonathan could give it to him. Something blue streaked past his eyes.

Jonathan gasped. Brewster's order for Austin Roe had been sealed with blue. He had given Levi Adams the wrong letter!

"Sir, I made a mistake," said Jonathan, trying to hold his voice steady. "That's the wrong letter. It's for someone else. Here, this is the letter for you." He pulled out the other letter and thrust it toward Adams, who grabbed it with a grunt.

"Please, sir. May I have the other one back?" asked Jonathan meekly. His heart was thudding wildly. It would not matter if he set up ten spy operations if he failed just once on a mission for Caleb Brewster. He had to get the letter back.

Adams tapped the point of his hunting knife against the two letters thoughtfully. Jonathan watched, afraid to speak again or even move. If only he could get both letters back. He did not want to get in on any spy operation that involved this crazy man. He just wanted to get out of there and never see Adams again.

Suddenly Levi Adams snapped to attention. He stuffed

both letters into his shirt and pointed the hunting knife directly at Jonathan.

Jonathan winced. The point glinted no more than two inches from his throat.

"Let it be a lesson to you not to make mistakes," Adams snarled. His bloodshot eyes gleamed hard and cold. "Now get outta here and leave me alone, you snot-nosed, chicken-breasted, bat-eared, squeaky-voiced *brat!*"

Chapter 7

Jonathan wanted to run. He wanted to get out of there so fast that Adams would wonder if he had ever really been there in the first place, but his legs refused to work. He had never felt so helpless in his life.

"Well!" thundered Levi Adams. He still held the knife pointed straight at Jonathan's throat.

"I . . . I can't, sir."

"What do you mean, you can't?"

"What I mean is . . ." Jonathan's mind raced, trying to think of an explanation. "What I mean is, you haven't read the letter from Bracy Gwinnett. He said I was to stay until you read it."

Adams eyed him suspiciously for a moment. Finally, with a sigh, he tossed the knife back onto the mantel and reached inside his shirt to draw out both of the letters. Jonathan let his breath out slowly, feeling as if his last ounce of energy were going with it. Still, he could not fall apart now, not while there was still a chance.

Sucking air in deeply, he held it until his chest ached as Adams laboriously read the letter from Gwinnett. It seemed to take forever, and Jonathan strained along with Adams as he slowly formed each word with his lips and now and then stopped and scratched his head with the corner of the letter for Austin Roe.

When Adams finally looked at Jonathan again, the scowl was gone from his face and Jonathan could scarcely believe the wheezy chuckle that he heard.

"So we're going to be partners, are we?" said Adams, shaking his head as if he could not believe his own words. "Not just ordinary partners, mind you, but *spy* partners. You and me and Bracy Gwinnett. Now if that don't beat all."

He slapped his leg and began to wheeze again, but he stopped abruptly a moment later. His face rumpled into a frown and he thrust the unopened letter toward Jonathan.

"Here. Take your letter," he said. "It won't do us any good to get started off on the wrong foot."

"Thank you, sir," said Jonathan. He took the letter and stuffed it into his shirt quickly so that Adams would not see that his hand was shaking.

"Now that we're partners, you can call me Levi," he said in a tone that was almost friendly.

"Yes, sir . . . I mean, Levi." Jonathan tried to relax and smile, but he could not completely shake off his uneasy feeling. "Guess I better be going."

"Tell Bracy that I think his idea's a good one and that I'll have something for you the next time you come to Long Island," said Levi as Jonathan moved toward the door. "Just one more thing. Next time, remember that you're a spy, and don't go around lookin' so scaredy."

Jonathan hesitated for an instant, feeling his ears turn red, and then hurried through the door. The goat looked at him soberly as he took off at a run, with Adams' wheezy laughter in his ears. How was he going to stand it being partners with a man like that?

Patting his shirt to make certain that the letter for Austin Roe was still there, Jonathan turned onto Old Field Road and headed toward Setauket. He was relieved that his mission for Bracy Gwinnett was over. Surely there was a better way of spying on the British than trusting a rum-sodden old ruffian like Levi Adams.

Maybe he could hang around the Roe Tavern for a while and listen to the conversations of the British officers. Better still, he could watch who came and went from the British headquarters in the Presbyterian church. He had to pass there on the way to the Roe Tavern, anyway. Surely he could find out something important if he kept his eyes and ears open.

The Presbyterian church on the village green looked as forlorn as ever, and Jonathan sauntered slowly through the grass searching for a spot that would give him the best vantage point. He decided on a tall elm tree standing near the road, partly because it gave him a good view of the stockade and the grounds as well as the church, and partly because its roots curled nest-like through the soft green grass, making a perfect place for him to rest.

A lone sentry paced back and forth in front of the

stockade. Otherwise, all was quiet at the church. The front doors were closed. Only the silent snouts of the swivel guns seemed to peer out of the windows. Jonathan shivered as he looked at the guns and wondered if a British soldier was stationed behind each one. And if there were soldiers behind the guns, were they watching him?

I really should have taken this letter to Austin Roe before I started spying, he thought nervously. After all, that was my real mission. He sighed and settled back in the cradle of roots. I'll just rest a few minutes and then I'd better go.

When Jonathan awoke, the sun was already in the afternoon sky. He sat up with a start and looked around. The sentry had changed and now at least half a dozen horses stood in the churchyard. Jonathan scarcely noticed. It did not matter now. He could not let it. He had not intended to go to sleep. Now it was late and he had not delivered the letter to Austin Roe.

He jumped up, checked again to make sure he still had the letter, and bounded off in the direction of the Roe Tavern. A picture flashed into his mind of the captain stomping back and forth in front of the willows waiting for his return, and he broke into a run. He reached the Roe Tavern completely out of breath.

Austin Roe was talking with a customer, so Jonathan stopped beside the front door to catch his breath. A moment later, to Jonathan's surprise, the innkeeper stood beside him. He was smiling as he gave Jonathan's hand a hearty shake.

"I've been looking for you all day," said Roe. "I hope you have something for me."

"Yes, an order for some . . . some stuff," said Jonathan with a half-embarrassed shrug. He pulled the letter from inside his shirt and handed it to the smiling Roe.

"Very good, lad. Tell the captain that I should have your 'stuff' for you in three days. Now won't you sit down and have a glass of buttermilk?"

"No, thank you. I'd better be getting back."

Jonathan hurried from the tavern. That had not taken very long. Perhaps if he hurried, Captain Brewster would not be upset that he had been gone so long.

He raced across the village green, glancing at the Presbyterian church out of the corner of his eye. It was quiet again. The horses that had been there a few minutes ago were gone. It had been a disappointing first try at being a spy. Still, Austin Roe had said that the order would be ready in three days. Perhaps he could try again then.

Jonathan slowed to a trot when he reached Old Field Road. There was no sense trying to run at breakneck speed all the way to Conscience Bay. The road was oddly deserted, and the only sound was the crunch of his shoes in the loose dirt. Not even the birds were singing.

Strange, he thought. It's almost too quiet.

The afternoon sun was hot on the back of his neck, so after a while he stopped in a patch of shade. Across the road was a small farmhouse. Wash fluttered on the clothesline and smoke curled softly from the chimney, but the front door was closed tightly in spite of the warmth of the day.

Something flickered at a window. What was that? Jonathan wondered. He looked quickly at the window, but the curtain was drawn. It must have been his imagination.

Jonathan hurried on, but he could not shake off his uneasy feeling. Something was wrong. Where was everybody? He had not seen a farmer in a single field that he had passed. The yards were deserted, too. Where were the children and dogs? He stopped and looked down the road behind him, but there was no one there, either. In the distance he could hear a dog barking almost frantically, but the sound was faint and far away, and soon that stopped, too, leaving silence hanging as heavy as smoke in the air around him.

I don't know what this is all about, but I'm getting out of here, thought Jonathan, taking off at a run. It was not far now to Conscience Bay and the safety of the waiting whaleboat. Maybe he should tell the captain about the deserted countryside and his eerie feeling. Still, it would be awfully hard to explain.

Jonathan rounded a bend in the road and stopped in his tracks. It was no wonder everyone had hidden indoors. Ahead of him, clip-clopping along the narrow, twisting road on great barrel-chested mounts, was a company of British soldiers in full battle dress. A large field cannon groaned along at the rear of the formation, and it took four foot soldiers pulling two drag ropes to move it down the road.

Ducking behind a tree, Jonathan scratched his curly head and tried to think. Where could they be going? They were headed toward Conscience Bay, but there was nothing out there except salt marshes and sea gulls . . . and Brewster's whaleboat! That was it. They were on their way to attack the whaleboat. He had to warn the captain, but how?

Jonathan peered around the tree. The company of soldiers was moving at a snail's pace, but it was approaching another bend in the twisting road. There would be undergrowth beside the road for a while yet before they reached the grassy marshlands near the bay. If he could only get around the soldiers and take cover in the scrub pine and brambles that grew in thick tangles scarcely more than inches from where they would pass, then he could get to Brewster in time to warn him. It was a terrible chance, but he would have to take it.

Jonathan took a deep breath and plunged into the thicket at the right side of the road. It seemed to be denser than the growth on the left, but Jonathan knew that at any moment that could change. He stumbled along as fast as he could, aware that he was making far too much noise, but he slowed down to tiptoe when patches of red became visible through the leaves. Jonathan tried to steady himself. The pounding of the horses' hooves was enough noise to drown out most of the sounds that he would make, but if he snapped a twig or shook the bushes, he might draw attention to himself.

He scanned each spot of ground before he let a foot rest there, and he held his breath as he eased his shoulders through the trembling branches. The soldiers were getting away from him. He was moving too slowly.

Jonathan stopped for an instant and gathered his courage. The growth was still thick, but he knew that it would not stay that way for long. He would have to run for it. There was an opening ahead, almost like a path. If he could stay on that he would be all right.

He took a last deep breath, ducked low, and propelled himself down the narrow trail. At his side, the hoofbeat was still a steady cadence. So far, at least, they did not know that he was there.

Suddenly a flock of blackbirds hurled themselves into the air like grapeshot. Jonathan froze. He did not even dare to breathe.

"Whoa!"

Jonathan closed his eyes and huddled on the ground listening as the hoofbeats stopped and the big cannon creaked to a halt.

"Private, dismount and check the bushes for whatever it was that startled those birds."

"Yes, sir."

Lying as still as he could, Jonathan heard the private thrash through the undergrowth, coming closer and closer to where he lay. Finally the thrashing stopped, and Jonathan opened one eye. A red-coated soldier was looking down at him.

Chapter 8

"It's just a boy," the British soldier shouted over his shoulder. He was hardly more than a boy himself, with hair almost as red as his coat, and he did not look at all the way an enemy ought to look. Then he turned to Jonathan and said in the clipped accent of the British, "You'd better get up. The captain will want to talk to you."

Jonathan stood up and brushed the dried grass and dirt off his clothes. He was not in the uniform of the Continental Army, and nobody but Levi Adams and Bracy Gwinnett knew that he was a spy, but still his heart was pounding and he walked forward on unsteady legs. These soldiers might not look like the enemy, but they were. What if the British captain asked him a trick question? What if he gave himself away? They would probably shoot him on the spot.

"Well, son. Just what did you think that you were doing?" asked the captain impatiently. He had dismounted and was leaning against the cannon. His clothes were dusty and he looked very tired.

"I . . . um . . . I . . ." Jonathan's mind was a blank, and he stared at the cannon, avoiding the captain's eyes. Surely there was some excuse that he could give for being in those bushes.

"Playing spy?" the captain snapped.

Jonathan jumped so hard that he nearly lost his balance. He was caught by the captain's steely gaze and he could not look away. The captain knew. There was no doubt about it. He knew that Jonathan was a spy. Rivers of perspiration poured down his face and he shifted his weight from one foot to the other. Clenching his fists, he took a deep breath before he spoke. "Yes, sir. That's what I was doing, all right. Tracking you and playing like I was a spy."

The captain regarded him sternly for what seemed to Jonathan like an eternity. He knows I'm lying, Jonathan thought. His jaws were starting to ache from gritting his teeth.

Finally the captain spat on the ground and growled, "Get on home and don't let me catch you at such foolishness again. You could get yourself killed!"

The anger in his eyes made Jonathan cringe. "Yes, sir. I'll be going along now," he said, and he took off down the road at a trot, heading back toward Setauket, afraid even to look behind.

When he had rounded a bend in the road and knew he was out of sight of the British soldiers, Jonathan stopped and fell to his knees in the dusty road. Tears filled his throat and spilled out of his eyes, and he

pounded the dirt with his fists. He had failed. Now there was no way to warn Brewster and the others that they were going to be attacked. Some soldier he was. Some spy.

There's no use going back to town, he thought. Even if I could get Levi Adams to help, it would be too late by the time we got back.

Jonathan got to his feet and scuffed slowly down the road toward Conscience Bay. I can't just desert. I've got to think of something! He started to run.

Ahead of him the cannon creaked faintly and the hoofbeats pounded like a distant drumbeat as the company of British soldiers got on its way again. Every step would take them closer to the unsuspecting whaleboat, while he trailed helplessly behind. If only he had not fallen asleep in front of the church. Then they might already be out in the Sound, far beyond the range of the enemy cannon.

It did not take Jonathan long to catch up with the soldiers again, and he darted from tree to tree, being careful to stay out of sight. At first it was easy. The mounted soldiers rode in perfect military order, with their backs straight and their eyes to the front. But the road suddenly grew bumpier, and the cannon crew had to turn around to steady the ammunition locker that rode between the long trails and to secure the ramrod in its rests.

Jonathan ducked behind a bush, certain that he had been seen. Surely they would shoot him if they caught him spying a second time. He held his breath, but the company of soldiers jogged on down the road without hesitation.

Just one more hill and they would reach the bay. The last farmhouse was far behind them, and sand dotted with clumps of beach grass spread out on either side of the road. The trees and bushes were stunted and sparse and growing farther and farther apart. Jonathan's heart pounded each time he had to race from one spot of cover to the next.

Suddenly, at the base of the hill, the captain reined in his horse and raised his arm as a signal for all to halt. Then he motioned them toward a small stand of scrub pine about thirty feet off the right side of the road. Jonathan peered cautiously through the thin foliage as the soldiers dismounted and tied their horses to the trees. The cannon, which was too wide to fit between the pines, was pulled up alongside.

A moment later a red-coated scout hurried up the hill. He flattened out when he reached the crest and put a long spyglass to his eye.

There was not much time left. The horse soldiers were clustering around the captain to wait for the return of the scout, but the cannon crew had already set to work. Jonathan swallowed hard as he watched one soldier take a bag of gunpowder out of the ammunition box and hand it to a second man, who pushed it down the barrel with the ramrod.

Jonathan squinted to see what went in next. It looked like a bag of grapeshot instead of a single cannon ball, but he could not be sure. His mind was whirling. Grape-shot would pelt a wide area, so that it was almost certain the whaleboat and her crew would be hit even if the British did not know the exact spot where she was hidden in the willows. He would have to stop them. But how?

Suddenly Jonathan saw his chance. The cannon crew had joined the others, and all eyes were on the scout at the top of the hill. Jonathan ducked as low as he could and ran, not seeing anything except the grove of trees directly ahead. He fell breathlessly onto a bed of pine needles and listened over the pounding of his heart to the soft murmur of voices. They had not seen him. Even the horses were undisturbed.

He raised his head slowly and looked around. He was a scant three feet from the cannon. Past the cannon he could see the soldiers still watching the scout, who had not moved from the crest of the hill.

Stretching out on his stomach, Jonathan inched toward the cannon. Its ugly snout was pointed toward the hill. Once it reached the crest, Brewster and his crew would not stand a chance.

Jonathan pulled himself up beside the cannon and ran a hand over the top of the barrel until he found the vent hole. Out of the corner of his eye he could see the scout, a dot of red, moving back down the hill. He knew all about how a cannon worked from watching the militia exercise in some of the towns where his father's wagon had stopped. But he would never have time. There was too much to do.

Frantically he searched along the side of the cannon for the powder horn. It was not there. He had to have it to prime the vent hole. Without gunpowder in the vent hole the sparks would never be able to ignite the powder bag deep inside the barrel.

He glanced back at the group of soldiers. The scout was beside them, gesturing with his hands. Any second they would be ready to move on.

I can't worry about being seen now, Jonathan thought, ducking under the cannon. The powder horn hung on the other side, and he grabbed it and scooted back again. He thrust its point into the vent hole and filled it with powder.

Now all that was left to do was to strike a spark. Surely there would be a flint in the ammunition box.

"Hey there! You! Get away from that cannon!"

Jonathan clenched his teeth. There was no turning back now. The soldiers were starting toward him. The ammunition box was too far away, so he grabbed a rock off the ground and scraped that against the opening to the vent hole.

"Come on! Spark!" he cried.

The soldiers had almost reached him. The captain opened his mouth to shout, but the sound was lost in the thunder of cannon fire and his face was hidden behind a flash of fire and smoke. As the tremendous boom echoed against the hillside, Jonathan sank against the shuddering cannon wheel. Brewster had been warned.

Chapter 9

There was not a second to lose. Jonathan ducked around the cannon wheel just ahead of the dazed British soldiers. He darted into the pines and grabbed the reins of the first horse that he came to. Vaulting into the saddle, he streaked out of the grove of trees and up the hill with the shouts of the redcoats at his back.

An instant later he heard the thunder of horses' hooves. They were after him. If only he could outrun them. And if only Brewster would be able to get the whaleboat safely away.

At last Jonathan reached the crest of the hill. Below, at the willow-lined shore, nothing stirred. There was no sign of life—no sign of Brewster or the *Spindrift* casting off, nothing. Had he already been warned?

Jonathan was seized with panic. Had the whaleboat already gone, leaving him alone with a company of British soldiers at his heels? Where would he go? What would he do? As the hooves pounded behind him, he dug his heels into the horse's flank and plunged down the hill toward the deserted shore.

He reined the horse up just short of the willows, stopping so abruptly that the horse reared and spilled him off backward. Jonathan scrambled to his feet, suddenly aware of a strange quietness. He looked up the hill, but the British had stopped midway and were staring silently in his direction.

"Barlowe. Get in the boat."

Jonathan whirled around. To his astonishment, he saw that the willows had been parted like a curtain around the whaleboat and that Caleb Brewster stood defiantly in the bow, pointing the swivel gun directly at the enemy.

The soldiers began backing their horses slowly up the hill, looking as if they were being pulled by invisible ropes. In the boat the crew was tense but ready with loaded muskets in their hands. All eyes were on the retreating British. Only the sound of the riderless horse cantering back up the hill broke the eerie stillness.

Jonathan stumbled to his place in the boat. He glanced at Bracy, expecting a reassuring grin, but Gwinnett did not even seem to see him. He was staring at the redcoated soldiers with a look of horror on his face.

I guess everybody gets scared except maybe Captain Brewster, Jonathan thought as he began to fumble with his musket. His hands were shaking so hard that he could scarcely load it.

The instant that the British disappeared behind the crest of the hill, Brewster gave the signal to cast off.

"Put your backs into it, men," he shouted as the crew began to row. "Those lobsterbacks'll take the road and try to cut us off on the sandspit at Old Field Point. If they do, we'll be as helpless as a beached whale. Pray that draggin' that cannon will slow 'em down enough for us to reach open water." He paused and stared for a moment at the deserted hillside. "Barlowe. Come here."

Jonathan stood up slowly. He did not want to face the captain. I've really done it this time, he thought. I led the British straight to the whaleboat.

Just then the boat left the sandy bank with a lurch, pitching Jonathan forward slightly, as if urging him toward Brewster. "Yes, sir," he said, stopping short beside the swivel gun.

"Why did the British fire their cannon before they crested the hill?" the captain asked with a frown.

"They didn't, sir. I fired it." Jonathan paused. There was a flicker of surprise in Brewster's stern eyes, so he went on, spilling out the words. "I sneaked up while they were busy talking to their scout and I fired it to warn you. I don't know how I did it; I just did."

"Good work, lad," said the captain. Then he dismissed Jonathan with a wave of his hand and turned back to his post in the bow.

Back at his place, Jonathan squinted against the glare of the late-afternoon sun on the water and tried to row. Was that the staccato beat of horses' hooves racing along a distant road that he heard, or was it his imagination? Fear lumped cold and hard in the pit of his stomach. He had not had time to be afraid before. Everything had happened too fast. But now it seemed that the whaleboat was frozen in the center of the bay, locked in a moment in time, and he could still smell the gunpowder from the cannon and hear the shouts of the soldiers as they had tried to stop his escape. He hung his head over the side of the boat and was sick.

Some soldier I am, he thought when he was able to sit up again a moment later, but no one had seemed to have noticed. The oarsmen moved like one body, forward, backward, forward again, to a beat set by the bumping of the oars against the oarlocks. The rhythm was soothing, and soon Jonathan had gripped his oar and begun the steady push and pull in time with the others. Only Brewster remained completely still, slumped against the swivel gun as he stared intently across the bay.

With each upward pull of the oar Jonathan glanced quickly at the shore. The *Spindrift* had almost reached Old Field Point, but he saw no signs of red-coated soldiers on the gray sandspit ahead. Had they stopped somewhere out of sight to reload the cannon, or were they still far off down the road?

Overhead a wheeling sea gull pierced the air with its screamlike cry and sent a shiver up Jonathan's back. He closed his eyes for a moment, wishing that when he opened them again he would see the Connecticut shore, but the deserted sandspit was still there. It seemed to be floating toward the boat. Its scattered clumps of reeds stood as silent as gravestones in the breathless air.

Finally the hull grazed the soft sand of the shore,

and the boat came to a stop. For an instant no one stirred. Then, as if guided by a silent command, the crew soundlessly stowed their oars, tied drag ropes to their oarlocks, and one by one dropped over the sides of the boat. Brewster stayed in the bow beside the swivel gun until everyone was out. Then he gave a last look around and joined the crew on the beach.

Jonathan stared across the sandspit. Last night, without the danger of attack from British soldiers, it had not seemed like a long distance to drag the boat. Now it looked a mile wide, even though the tide was high and had narrowed the finger of land to be crossed to thirty or forty yards at the most. The sun teetered like a red ball on the edge of the horizon. Soon the fading light of dusk would blur shapes and colors. Only the large hull of the whaleboat would be easy to spot.

Getting a firm grip on his drag rope, Jonathan began to pull. The faster they got the boat to open water, the sooner the danger would be past.

There was no sound except the shush of the boat as it moved across the sand. It's like a dream, Jonathan thought, looking ahead at the long line of dark forms bent low and straining at the ropes.

"Fire!"

The silence exploded into a nightmare of musket fire. Jonathan dived into the sand and rolled as close as he could to the hull of the boat. All around him the reeds were alive with the red flare of exploding gunpowder, tiny suns flashing in the deepening dusk.

He tried to think. His musket was in the boat. He was

77

in the open, an easy target. He rolled his eyes from side to side, afraid to move even his head, and looked for some place to go.

"Into the boat!" Brewster ordered. The scrambling thuds of men going over the wooden sides was a dull echo to the gunfire.

He had to get up. He knew it. He had to stand up and crawl into the boat, but he lay in the sand paralyzed with fear. The whaleboat shuddered as the swivel gun discharged, and above him the crewmen returned the musket fire. That would give him cover. Now was the time to go.

Still he could not move. He rolled over on his stomach and pushed up onto his knees. Breathlessly he tried to stand up, but instead he froze. Crouched in the sand not ten feet away was a British soldier. Cocking the firelock of his musket, he leveled the barrel straight at Jonathan's head.

There was a thunder of gunfire and a scream and something fell on top of him. An instant later he felt himself being jerked upward, his shoulders protesting in their sockets. Then he crashed down into the wooden bottom of the boat.

"Well, Jonny my friend. Thought you might like to join us."

Jonathan looked up into Bracy Gwinnett's smiling face, aware for the first time that the musket fire had not been the British soldier's and that the scream had not been his own.

"You . . . you saved my life," he whispered.

Gwinnett thrust the Brown Bess into Jonathan's hand and set to work, reloading his own musket without a word.

Jonathan watched him a moment and found himself beginning to tremble. Bracy could have been killed a few moments ago, and now he was acting as if nothing had happened. He was a real friend. Jonathan turned and peered over the side of the boat. The reeds stood deathly still, and there was only an occasional burst of gunfire from the British.

Darkness had fallen and the moon was caught behind a cloud. Jonathan rested his chin on an arm and drew a long, deep breath. Maybe the British were retreating. Maybe it was almost over.

He did not have long to rest. Brewster knelt beside an injured crewman for a moment and then moved to the center of the boat.

"Men," he said, motioning for the crew to gather around him. "My guess is that the cavalry came on ahead and that the cannon will be here any minute. They're probably reassembling now to try to knock us off before we reach the water. Our swivel gun's no match for their four-pounder. We've gotta outrun 'em."

A shiver raced up Jonathan's spine. He had forgotten all about the cannon. As if on cue, his ears caught the faint sound of the creak of heavy wheels.

Chapter 10

The night suddenly became bright as the veil of tattered clouds that had seemed snagged against the face of the moon moved swiftly aside. Jonathan stiffened in the silver light and looked out of the corner of his eye at the spot where the road from Setauket ended and the narrow sandspit began. There sat the British cannon perched like a vulture on top of a sandy rise no more than fifty yards away.

The cannon crew was working feverishly. How could the *Spindrift* possibly reach open water before the cannon was aimed, then loaded and primed for firing?

Without waiting for Brewster's command, the sailors slid over the side of the boat and grabbed their drag ropes.

Jonathan shivered. The British soldiers worked almost soundlessly as they prepared for their attack. Only the grunts of the straining crewmen punctuated the silence.

Jonathan's lungs were bursting. The rope cut into

his hands and pressed painfully against his shoulder. He tightened his grip and dug into the sand with each step forward. The water was only inches away.

Blood pounded against his temples like shock waves from an exploding cannon. Any second now it would happen. Any instant the whaleboat would be blown to bits. Jonathan felt icy water rising above his ankles, then above his knees. He could hear Packett shouting orders, but his mind was too blurred to distinguish the words. The salty sting of water on his bleeding hands brought him back to consciousness and he scrambled into the boat and picked up his oar.

"Row!" cried Packett from the tiller. "Row!"

There was a volley of musket fire from the beach. Jonathan ducked his head as he pulled on the oar with all his strength. Something flashed in the bow of the boat, and he looked up again just as the swivel gun discharged.

Then it came—the roar that he had been waiting for rolling like thunder across the water. Jonathan closed his eyes and hugged his oar and waited.

"Keep rowing!" Packett shouted, but Jonathan could not move.

"Why doesn't it hit?" he whispered through trembling lips. "What's taking it so long?"

Jonathan heard a low whine as something passed over the boat and then a splash several feet off starboard. The British had overshot their mark. He opened his eyes and began to row as Captain Brewster returned the fire with the swivel gun. The redcoats had missed once, but they would reload and fire again. He put all his strength behind his oar, knowing that the other crewmen were doing the same, but it seemed as if the *Spindrift* were standing still. How could they possibly get away in time? Push. Pull. Push. Pull. Sea gulls, routed from their sleep by the battle, screamed in the air above the whaleboat as if to warn the sailors of the danger.

Suddenly it came again. The shattering boom of the cannon filled the air, and Jonathan gripped his oar with a greater burst of strength than he had ever felt before.

The cannonball whizzed overhead once more and sank into the water only inches past the boat. They were getting closer. They had barely missed this time.

It took minutes to clean and reload a cannon, but it had seemed more like seconds between the first two shots, and Jonathan listened tensely for the sound that he knew would come again. Push. Pull. Push. Pull. There was nothing else to do. If only he could look around and see what was going on and how far away from shore they were. His stomach was churning, and he felt as if he were going to be sick again, but he kept his head low and tried to concentrate on his oar.

Finally a third blast pierced the air. His heart was pounding wildly and sweat poured down his face. Surely they would not miss this time. Then suddenly he heard a splash off the port side of the boat. There was a sigh almost in unison from the crew. The *Spindrift* was finally out of range.

"Well, Jonny my friend, looks like we made it without a scratch." Bracy wore his usual ear-to-ear grin, and Jonathan smiled weakly and tried to speak, but the words were not yet ready to come. Bracy nodded as if he understood and continued to row in silence.

The rest of the crew was silent, too. Each one's busy thinking about how close he just came, thought Jonathan, fighting to hold back the tears of relief that choked his throat and welled up in his eyes.

Still, he could not help wondering why no one but he had been scared through all of it. Brewster had stood exposed and unflinching in the bow of the boat and fired the swivel gun at the enemy. The other crewmen had climbed into the boat in the midst of gunfire while he lay whimpering on the ground. And Bracy, his good friend, had taken a chance on being killed himself in order to save Jonathan's life. Why were all of them so brave and he so afraid? He was grown up now, free and independent, answering to no one, wasn't he? But even Levi Adams had said that he looked "scaredy."

Jonathan worked his oar in rhythm with the others and thought about Levi Adams. It would take an awful lot of courage to go back to that house again. If Adams was in another of his drunken tantrums, there was no telling what he might do. How was he going to explain all that to Bracy without sounding like a coward? After all, Bracy had just saved his life. How was he going to tell him that he did not want to be a spy?

There was no sound now except the gentle lapping of waves against the boat, and Jonathan fought to hold off the drowsiness that was settling over him like fog. He would have to think about it later, when his mind was clear.

A few hours later Jonathan sank into his bed at Mrs. Hoad's boardinghouse without so much as taking off his shoes. Across the room Bracy snuffed out the candle, and Jonathan heard the feather mattress sigh as Bracy, too, fell into bed. They had walked home from Black Rock Harbor practically in silence, both too exhausted for conversation. Bracy had asked Jonathan if he had delivered the letter to Levi Adams and Jonathan had answered yes and had left it at that for the time being. The two had dropped into bed without so much as exchanging good-nights. Jonathan turned on his side. Delicious sleep was just a breath away.

The instant his eyelids closed, the leering face of Levi Adams bobbed into his mind. He did not want to think about Adams. All he wanted was to go to sleep. There would be plenty of time in the morning to decide what he was going to say to Bracy and then say it. Now he had to get some sleep.

But it seemed to Jonathan as if the old ruffian's picture was glued to the insides of his eyelids, because no matter what he did he could not make it go away.

Finally, in disgust, he got out of bed. I may as well get this over with, he thought, and he crossed the dark room to Bracy's bed.

"Are you asleep?" he asked softly.

"Yup," Bracy said thickly. "So go away."

"I can't go to sleep until I talk to you about something," Jonathan insisted.

"Try."

"I did."

"Try harder."

"It's about Levi Adams," said Jonathan.

There was a rustle of bedclothes, and a moment later candlelight flared from a nearby table. All traces of sleepiness were gone from Bracy's face, and he eyed Jonathan solemnly for a moment before asking, "What about him? You did see him, didn't you, and give him my letter?"

"Sure, I did all that, but . . . well . . ." Jonathan was still uncertain about how to begin. "How long has it been since you've seen your cousin?"

"A long time. Why?"

"Seems to me he's gone a bit past being just a ruffian with peculiar ways. I'd say he's worked all the way up to crazy," said Jonathan, and then he poured out the story of his visit to Adams' house.

Bracy was doubled over with laughter before Jonathan had finished his story. "That's old Levi, all right," he said, slapping his thigh. "Trying to get your goat. Looks like he got it, too. Why, how do you think he fools the British all the time? Think they pay any mind to a blustery old drunk like him?"

"I suppose not," said Jonathan sheepishly.

"Now go to sleep," said Bracy, blowing out the candle again. "We'll talk about it some more in the morning."

This time sleep came easily. Dreamlessly Jonathan drifted down dark corridors. Deeper. Deeper. Then suddenly an explosion ripped into his consciousness. Cannon fire! Over and over again! He had to run . . . get to safety.

Jonathan bolted upright and opened his eyes. There was no cannon. He had only been dreaming. But before he could sink back onto his pillow he heard it again. Pounding. Hammering. Someone was beating on the door to his room.

"Who is it?" he called out.

"Brewster. Is that you, Barlowe? Get out here on the double."

Jonathan sprang out of bed and raced toward the door.

"Bracy," he whispered in the darkness, but there was no answer except a wheezy snore.

As soon as Jonathan was out in the hallway, Brewster headed down the stairway and out the door. Jonathan hurried behind him. Outside, the captain's big stallion pranced nervously, eager for a gallop. Brewster mounted and reined him up tightly. Then he extended a hand toward Jonathan.

Jonathan stifled a surprised gasp and heaved himself up onto the horse's rump behind the captain. The flat saddle afforded no handhold, so he grabbed the captain's coat just as the horse jolted forward and thundered into the night.

Where were they going? He was afraid to hope that Brewster was taking him on a special mission. The captain had said nothing when he offered an arm up. Jonathan clung to Brewster as the pounding hooves drowned out the night sounds and blackness was everywhere. They were heading away from the town—north, as best Jonathan could judge—and Brewster, head bent over the reins, seemed determined to get there in a hurry.

Presently he slowed the horse to a trot and sat tall in the saddle, alert to every sound. Jonathan stiffened too. What was the captain looking for? Trouble?

"Who goes there?"

Jonathan jerked to the left toward the direction from which the man's voice had come, but Brewster remained unflinching in the saddle.

"Captain Caleb Brewster, here, and a private, Jonathan Barlowe,'" replied Brewster calmly.

"What say you to 'industry'?" demanded the hidden sentry.

"I say 'wealth.' "

"You may pass."

A moment later they entered a clearing, and Brewster called back over his shoulder, "This is the camp of Major Benjamin Tallmadge's Second Regiment of Light Dragoons. Look sharp. Don't forget that you're a soldier even though you aren't in uniform."

Jonathan caught his breath as he looked out across a field to his right where dozens of pale tents stood in the moonlight. Most of them were small wall tents, interspersed with a few larger fly tents. In the center of the camp was a large oval marquee with a scalloped roof and a pair of sentries at the entrance flap. Horses, tethered at one side of the camp, stirred restlessly as the captain and Jonathan approached the marquee, and low-burning bonfires fluttered in the slight breeze. All else was still.

Jonathan slid to the ground the moment the horse stopped. One of the sentries had disappeared, but by the time the captain had dismounted and brushed the dust from his coat the sentry had reappeared from inside the tent. "You may both go in now," he said.

The tent flap raised slowly from inside, and in the soft glow of candlelight Jonathan saw a strikingly handsome man. He was tall and thin with a hawkish face, and his smile was warm as he returned the captain's salute.

"Welcome, Cale. Come in . . . both of you." Major Tallmadge stepped back to allow them to enter.

The two men seemed to forget that Jonathan was there, and he stared after them as they hurried to the far end of the huge tent, where the major's desk stood, and spoke together in whispered tones. Jonathan still had no idea why the captain had brought him along, and he felt awkwardly conspicuous as he stood alone and ignored at the front of the tent. Perhaps he should have followed them to the desk.

Jonathan fidgeted, shifting from one foot to the other, and surveyed the tent. Along one wall a pair of campaign trunks flanked a folding camp bed, and on one of the trunks a small mantel clock ticked noisily. On the other side of the marquee stood the major's mess chest and three camp stools. Except for the desk and the camp stools, on which the men sat, there was no other furniture in the tent.

The voices droned on monotonously and Jonathan strained to read the clock, but the shadows around it were too deep. He scanned the room for something else to look at, something to do while he waited. There was nothing. He sighed and listened to the relentless ticking of the clock.

Jonathan's eyelids began to droop, and he tried to recall when he had last slept a night through. The tent was stuffy, and his thoughts were becoming foggy. He planted his feet wide and locked his knees stiffly to try to hold himself erect as he fought harder and harder against sleep. Slowly his eyes closed. He could see the scalloped waves of the Sound rising and falling in endless succession, and he could hear them slapping gently against the hull of the *Spindrift*. He could feel her rocking cradlelike as she drifted away from the shore. . . .

"Barlowe!"

The word lashed him like a sudden squall. It stopped his breath and jolted him off balance so that when he opened his eyes the roof of the tent spun above him.

Chapter 11

Jonathan staggered to his feet. "Look sharp. Don't forget that you're a soldier." The captain's words burned in his ears. What must Brewster think of him now? Was everything he ever did going to end in humiliation?

"Major Tallmadge would like a word with you," said Brewster. He motioned for Jonathan to approach the desk, and then ducked out through the tent flap into the night.

Jonathan pulled himself up to his full height and marched slowly and steadily toward the major, but inside he was sick at heart. They think I'm a babe, he thought. They don't want me in their army. I'm going to be discharged.

Jonathan avoided Tallmadge's eyes as he saluted, focusing on the spotless white facings and buttons that edged the major's deep-blue coat. Spotless, too, was the empty white sword belt that crossed from shoulder to hip. Jonathan winced as he thought of his own clothes, rumpled and dirty from two nights in a whale-boat and a day spent tramping along a dusty road.

"Congratulations on your bravery today," said the major. Jonathan looked up, startled, as Tallmadge went on. "Captain Brewster tells me that you set off a British cannon to warn him and his crew of an impending attack."

"Yes, sir," said Jonathan proudly. He could feel the blood rising in his face and knew that his ears must be turning red. "Thank you, sir."

"Why did you enlist, Private Barlowe?" Major Tall-madge asked kindly. "Ordinarily fourteen is a little young."

"Begging your pardon, sir, but age had nothing to do with it. You see, my folks are all dead, so I'm on my own and I can do what I please. I'm free and in-dependent, answering to no one."

"And that's why you enlisted? I don't quite under-stand."

"Well, sir. I figure that that's what America wants, too—to be free and independent, I mean—and I want to help her."

"Freedom and independence are wonderful gifts," Major Tallmadge said almost sadly. "The problem for man and country alike is knowing how to use them wisely."

Jonathan nodded. He was beginning to feel more at ease.

"I understand that Captain Brewster entrusted you

to carry out two special missions. Will you tell me about the first one?"

"Yes, sir. I went into Setauket, Long Island, to the Roe Tavern and got a loaf of bread." Jonathan could feel the color rising in his face again, but this time it was from embarrassment rather than pride. It was bad enough that he had had to do it, but admitting it to someone like Major Tallmadge was even worse.

"Were those your exact instructions?" the major asked.

"No, sir. I was told to speak to Austin Roe and only to him and to ask for a package for John Bolton."

"And this package turned out to be merely a loaf of bread?"

"Yes, sir," said Jonathan with a trace of irritation.

"What was the second mission you carried out for the captain?"

"I delivered a letter to Austin Roe. Captain Brewster said it was an order for some stuff he needed."

"And what were your exact instructions that time?"

"To take the letter to Austin Roe and to conduct my business with no one but Austin Roe himself."

"And that's precisely what you did?"

"Yes, sir."

"You did not speak to another person either in Setauket or on the road?"

"No, sir," Jonathan said slowly. For an instant he had the feeling that he was being questioned by his father, who had always seemed to know when he was lying. Was it possible that Major Tallmadge knew about Levi Adams and that Jonathan had disobeyed the captain's order?

Major Tallmadge paused. When he spoke again his voice was barely above a whisper, and his slow, deliberate words had a deadly seriousness about them that sent a shiver up Jonathan's spine.

"Then I have your assurance that you have no idea how the British knew that Captain Brewster and the *Spindrift* were hiding in the willows at Conscience Bay?"

Jonathan was stunned. Could he have betrayed them himself? He certainly had not meant to. But it wasn't hard for him to believe that Levi Adams would sell out his own cousin for a bottle of rum.

Jonathan dared not give himself away, so he cleared his throat and tried to hide the flicker of fear that he was certain had been in his eyes. "I have no idea how they found out, sir," he said as steadily as he could.

The major was silent for what seemed like an eternity, and he stared hard at Jonathan, as though by looking into his eyes he could see straight into his soul. Finally he spoke. "All right, Private. I believe you, and I have something very important to tell you—something that you must not repeat to anyone."

Major Tallmadge paused again, as if he could scarcely bring himself to say the words.

"I suppose that it will surprise you to learn that the loaf of bread that you delivered to the captain contained a secret letter and that Austin Roe, John Bolton, and Captain Brewster are in the private service of General Washington?"

"The private service of General Washington? What's that?"

"Spies, Private Barlowe. Spies!"

"Spies?" whispered Jonathan, unable to believe what he had just heard.

"The letter that you carried to Austin Roe today was General Washington's reply to the letter in the loaf of bread."

Jonathan caught his breath. He had carried a letter written by General Washington himself and he had not known it. What if Levi Adams had kept it, after all?

The major's voice cut into his thoughts. "There's a man in the city of New York who lives in mortal danger every day of his life. His code name is Samuel Culper, and no one except General Washington knows who he really is. Culper moves freely among the officers of the British High Command whose headquarters is in New York. He listens to bits of conversation—a word dropped here, a question there. He hears many things, such as where British troops are being placed, what ships will be passing through Long Island Sound, and what new attacks are being planned."

A shiver ran through Jonathan as he tried to imagine himself making conversation with British officers, smiling, and all the while listening for military secrets.

"Culper puts this intelligence information into coded

messages and sends them along a secret route to General Washington."

"A secret route?"

"The network of spies that passes the messages from New York City to Long Island to my camp here in Connecticut and finally to General Washington himself. Do you have any questions about what I've said so far?"

Jonathan took a deep breath and gazed at the floor. In his mind he could see men with blurred faces meeting in dark alleyways, exchanging secret papers, thundering through the night on jet-black stallions. He wanted to hear more,

"No, sir," he said, pulling himself up as straight as he could and meeting the major's eyes.

"As you already know, Captain Brewster's portion of the secret route lies across the Devil's Belt from Setauket to this camp."

Major Tallmadge paused and regarded Jonathan solemnly. Jonathan did not break away from the major's gaze.

"You were in Setauket and you saw the enemy soldiers. You saw what they have done to the Presbyterian church."

Jonathan nodded.

"There is great danger in Setauket to anyone who is not loyal to the crown. Caleb Brewster was born there, and his family still lives no more than a quarter mile from the Roe Tavern. He is well known, so you can see how dangerous it is for him to go into town to pick

up the intelligence even when it's hidden in something as simple as a loaf of bread. And it's equally dangerous for anyone from town to bring it out to his boat. Captain Brewster's idea of having you carry the messages seemed like a perfect solution. Ordinarily a fourteen-year-old boy going in and out of town would scarcely be noticed by the British Army."

"That must have been what the captain meant when he told Mr. Packett that he was letting me enlist because there was lots of good use to be made of a lad. Those were the exact words that he used. I thought he just wanted an errand boy."

Major Tallmadge smiled kindly. "And now you know that what he really wanted was a spy. He couldn't tell you then, because he had to be certain that a four-teen-year-old was man enough to carry out orders," said the major. Then he added sadly, "But now that you've proved yourself, you've been seen by an entire company of British soldiers."

Suddenly Jonathan felt very small standing in front of the major's desk. He had heard things tonight that could carry him beyond his grandest dreams. In the private service of General Washington, the major had called it. Spying was what it meant, and he, Jonathan Barlowe, had been a real spy. But as proud as he was at that moment, he could not forget how close he had come to bringing disaster down on all of them.

"You may wonder why I took the chance of telling you all this if your spy career is over," said the major.

"But the truth of the matter is that even though there is great danger now, you're still the best risk that we have for carrying out this essential operation."

Jonathan took a slow, deep breath. He was going to get a second chance.

"I want to do it, sir. I want to very much."

Major Tallmadge sighed wearily. "There's one more thing that I want to tell you before you make your decision," he said. "There was another young spy once. His name was Nathan Hale, His home was Coventry, Connecticut, but I met him while we both were students at Yale and he became my very closest friend. After graduation he took a position as a schoolmaster, but at the outbreak of the war he enlisted in the Continental Army. In September of 1776, disguised as a simple schoolmaster, he went behind the British lines on Long Island to discover their plans for attacking New York."

Major Tallmadge paused. There was a sad look in his eyes as he went on. "On September twenty-first he was caught while trying to make his way back through New York to his own lines. The next morning he was hanged without benefit of a trial or the comfort of a Bible. Nathan Hale was only nineteen."

Jonathan shivered. Nineteen was terribly young to die, and he was only fourteen, but he had to take the chance. He straightened his shoulders and met Major Tallmadge's eyes. "I'm sorry, sir . . . about your friend. But it doesn't change my mind. I want to be a spy."

Chapter 12

When Jonathan awoke in his own bed late the next afternoon, he lay there for a long time staring at the ceiling, certain that the meeting with Major Tallmadge had been just a dream. Surely a fourteen-year-old orphan and errand boy for Captain Caleb Brewster was not in the private service of General Washington. Not a spy. Not a real one.

But with the sudden memory of Levi Adams' treachery, Jonathan knew that it had not been a dream. He sat up quickly. He had to talk to Bracy.

The coverlets were neatly folded on Bracy's bed and the pillow plumped and in its place, but Bracy was gone. It's no wonder, Jonathan thought as he climbed out of his own bed. I've slept away most of the day.

He looked around the room for a note or some other clue to where Bracy had gone, but there was nothing.

Jonathan washed his face and changed into clean clothes. He would go looking for Bracy. There was no other choice.

His stomach grumbled hungrily, but he left the boardinghouse without stopping in the kitchen. He could not spare the time. Besides, Mrs. Hoad had made it plain at the beginning that she only fed boarders at mealtime.

Perhaps Bracy had gone to the beach. Jonathan took off at a sprint and arrived there out of breath. He looked up and down, but his friend was nowhere in sight. The sand was deserted.

The tide had retreated far into the Sound, leaving behind glinting tide pools and rocks frosted white with barnacles. Jonathan walked slowly toward the water's edge, sidestepping an exposed blue-mussel bed whose inhabitants lay frozen in openmouthed surprise that their cozy blanket of water had been snatched away. A gull shadow kited silently across the wet sand, and offshore an entire fleet of sea gulls rode the swells that were beginning to form as the tide, heeding the silent command of the moon, drifted back toward shore.

Jonathan shivered, remembering the night that he had walked along this same stretch of beach and had come upon the icy corpse of Bracy's fishing partner, Zeke. He had felt grown up then, ready to take on responsibility. He had been free and independent, answering to no one.

The sun was low in the cloudless sky, but it seemed small and dull and he scarcely needed to shade his eyes from its thin rays. Where could Bracy be? Where else would he go? Jonathan was beginning to feel uneasy, and he glanced quickly back over his shoulder, but there was nothing there except the gray-green water whispering secrets to the shore.

Jonathan squinted and tried to bring into focus a long blurred line far down the beach. It looked almost as if someone had laid a length of rope from the water's edge all the way up to where the sand gave way to grass and scrubby trees, but it was too far away for him to be sure. As he got closer, he could see that it was not a rope at all, but a sort of track. Something had been dragged out of the water and taken at least as far as the clumps of beach grass above.

Jonathan hurried over to the groove and saw that it was freshly made and deep. Whatever the object had been, it had been heavy. He looked up and down the beach once more. Still there was no one in sight. Slowly he followed the track up the sandy rise and into the grass. It was harder to see now, but it was still there.

Jonathan stopped abruptly. The track had ended at a long hole, about two feet deep, in the sandy dirt. Waves of dread washed over him. It was long and narrow like a grave, and it was empty. Whatever or whoever had been buried there had been dragged *into* the water instead of out of it.

Dropping to his knees, Jonathan stared into the empty grave. Bracy had buried Zeke somewhere near here.

Jonathan tried to push the thought out of his mind— but how many graves could there be along one stretch of beach? He stood up. The beach was still deserted, although out in the Sound a black speck was slowly growing larger against the late afternoon sky.

Jonathan watched as it turned from a speck to a blob and finally to a boat with a lone man at the oars.

I should get out of here, he thought, but instead he ducked behind a squat bramble bush and watched. He had to find out who was in the boat. It approached slowly, cutting the water with sharklike grace.

Jonathan still could not make out the features of the man, but he appeared tall and lean as he rowed rhythmically toward the beach. Jonathan looked away, not really wanting to see who it was. By the time he could make himself look again the boat was close to shore, and there was no mistaking the fact that the man was Bracy Gwinnett.

He dug up Zeke and dumped him in the Sound. But why? Jonathan shook his head back and forth, as if that simple movement would help him believe such an incredible thing. Maybe I'm wrong. Maybe it's just a stupid coincidence.

But Jonathan knew that it was not just a coincidence, and he watched Bracy row the boat straight toward the spot where the groove in the sand met the water. He jumped lightly out of the boat and dragged it up onto the sand. Then he scanned the beach carefully in every direction. Jonathan held his breath and stayed completely still. He did not want Bracy to see him. Not now. Not until he understood what Bracy was up to.

Using the flat side of an oar from the rowboat, Gwinnett advanced slowly up the beach and smoothed away the sandy track. Closer and closer he came. When he reached the grave site, Jonathan crouched stone-still behind the bush, afraid even to blink. Bracy quickly filled up the grave and gave one last look around before he bounded down the sand and pushed the rowboat back into the water. He turned the boat toward Black Rock Harbor and rowed away, leaving the beach looking as if it had never been disturbed.

Jonathan stared after the rowboat until it disappeared around a jetty. Then he turned and scuffed slowly back toward town. Nothing made sense anymore. He had believed that Captain Brewster thought he was a babe and had used him as an errand boy, when really the captain had made him into a spy. Bracy had trusted his cousin Levi Adams to help them set up their own spy operation, but Levi had betrayed them to the British. Now Bracy, who was the only person that he could turn to, had secretly dug up the body of the man he said had been his fishing partner and had dropped him into the sea. Why? What did it all mean? Was Gwinnett mixed up in something, too?

Bracy returned to the boardinghouse just before supper. Sporting his usual grin, he strode into the room he and Jonathan shared.

"Well, Jonny my friend. I see you finally decided to get up."

"I couldn't sleep through all the meals, now could I?" said Jonathan, trying to sound at ease.

"Well, you sure didn't sleep through the night. What happened to you? I woke up before dawn and you were gone."

"Captain Brewster came for me and took me to be questioned by Major Tallmadge of the second Regiment of Light Dragoons."

"Questioned? And by a major? What in heaven's name for?"

Jonathan paused to choose his words carefully. "He wanted to know if I had talked to anyone while I was in Setauket . . . anyone who could have tipped off the British about the whaleboat being in the willows at Conscience Bay."

"Well, did you?" asked Bracy impatiently.

"Only Levi Adams."

Bracy stiffened and looked at Jonathan sharply. "What are you trying to say?"

"What I'm trying to say is that that old buzzard gave us away. Bracy, face it, he probably sold us out for a stinking bottle of rum."

"I tell you he didn't," shouted Bracy. His face was flushed with anger. "I don't know how the British knew we were there. Maybe they didn't. Maybe they were just looking around, until you showed up and set off their cannon, and then rode right straight down the hill toward the boat. Maybe you gave us away yourself. Have you thought about that?"

Jonathan was stunned. Was it possible that what Bracy said was true? Maybe the British sent a patrol to the bay area every so often just to look around. Maybe he had risked his life to endanger the captain and the crew rather than to save them. He could not believe it. He would not.

Squaring his shoulders, he looked Bracy straight in the eye. "I did what I thought was best. There was no one around to ask," he said.

"Of course you did," said Bracy. His tone had softened and the smile had returned to his face. "I just wanted you to see that there were other possibilities. I don't believe that you tipped off the British, any more than I believe Levi tipped them off. He'll prove it to you himself the next time you contact him."

"There isn't going to be a next time. I'm finished with spying."

"Finished!" cried Bracy, clamping his hands on Jonathan's shoulders and facing him squarely. "I tell you, Levi Adams is on our side."

"It isn't just that," said Jonathan, avoiding Bracy's eyes.

"Then what is it?"

Jonathan hesitated. He couldn't tell Bracy the real reason, that he was already a spy, or that even if Levi Adams could be trusted there wasn't anything he could find out that General Washington didn't already know.

"Maybe the captain was right," said Bracy slowly. "Maybe you *are* just a babe if you turn coward after one close call."

"I'm not a coward," cried Jonathan. "And I'm not a babe!"

"Then why don't you want to spy?"

Suddenly a bell rang in the hall downstairs. "It's time for supper," said Jonathan sullenly. He took advantage of the interruption to brush past Bracy and clatter down to the dining room before the argument could continue.

At the table he avoided meeting Bracy's eyes, and he was glad when Mrs. Hoad engaged him in conversation.

"Seems like I didn't find out much about you, young man, when you first came here," she said. "Who did you say your folks were?"

"My father was the itinerant tailor who died out at the Gladdens' place a while back," said Jonathan. He was still angry but he hoped his voice sounded natural when he spoke to Mrs. Hoad. It must have, because she responded with a sympathetic nod. "I don't have any family now," Jonathan went on, "so I joined the army to fight for freedom and independence."

Mrs. Hoad smiled and turned to Bracy. "I know you're not from around here, either," she said.

"My fishing boat foundered in a storm in the Sound. It was my home and my livelihood as well. Now it's gone," said Bracy. "Why do you ask?"

An uncertain smile flickered over Mrs. Hoad's wrinkled face. "Not that I really thought it was you, of course," she said, "but people have been telling me that two Tories escaped from Newgate Prison up north of here a fortnight ago and that they were last seen heading for Long Island Sound. I just wanted to reassure myself."

"Escaped from Newgate Prison?" said Jonathan, giving a low whistle of disbelief.

Jonathan knew about Newgate Prison. In fact, he had even seen it. It was just over a year ago that his father's wagon had stopped in the town of Simsbury in northern Connecticut for a week or two. While his father was busy stitching a coat for a gentleman named Rufus Clay, Jonathan had become friends with Clay's son Benjie. Benjie had taken him to see Newgate Prison, and they had lain hidden in the bushes outside the high stone wall with its bastion, moat, and guard tower, while Benjie whispered its terrible secrets.

According to Benjie, Newgate Prison had once been a copper mine, and the prisoners were kept, not in the buildings visible aboveground, but in rat-infested dungeons in the same slimy pit from which the copper had once been dug. The only entrance to the honeycomb of dungeons deep inside the earth was through two iron-bolted trapdoors, the heaviest of which had to be hoisted with a tackle. And there was no escape.

And yet here sat Mrs. Hoad saying that two men *had* escaped from that awful place. Two men, and they had headed for Long Island Sound in a boat.

Jonathan looked at Bracy out of the corner of his eye. He did not like what he was thinking. Bracy had said that he and Zeke were fishermen, and Jonathan had had no reason not to believe him. And yet, why was he so thin? And why did his skin have the pasty paleness of someone who had not seen sunshine for a long time?

When they had returned to their room later, Bracy tossed back his head and laughed heartily. "Now I suppose you think Zeke and me are the Tories who broke out of Newgate?"

"Of course not," said Jonathan, but he knew that he

did not sound convincing. That would explain why Bracy had put Zeke where nobody could ever find him or know for sure who he was.

Bracy shook his head slowly. "Well, it would be a mighty strange Tory who would join the Continental Army," he said.

Bracy's words hit Jonathan like a thunderbolt. It *would* be a mighty strange Tory who would join the Continental Army—unless he was a spy. Jonathan closed his eyes. Levi Adams. The company of British soldiers at Conscience Bay. He did not want to think about it, but he could not stop.

Chapter 13

When the *Spindrift* left Black Rock Harbor a few hours later, Jonathan's mind was still reeling. If what he suspected was true, he would have to warn Captain Brewster. It was his responsibility as a soldier and as a man.

Still, he had no proof. What if he was wrong? After all, he owed his very life to Bracy Gwinnett.

Bracy had not mentioned either Levi Adams or the escaped Tories on the way to the boat. In fact, he had been his usual cheery self, and that had only deepened Jonathan's confusion. He wished he knew Bracy better and that he understood more of what went on behind that ready smile.

Jonathan glanced toward the bow of the boat. Captain Brewster leaned against the swivel gun, peering tensely into the blackness.

He never relaxes, Jonathan thought. He never rests or closes his eyes even for an instant.

Jonathan felt his face flush as he remembered how he had fallen asleep under the tree in Setauket and then again in Major Tallmadge's tent. Caleb Brewster would never have done that. And if he told the captain about Bracy, he would have to tell about himself, too. He would have to admit that he had disobeyed the captain's orders and had not only been responsible for the British attack on the whaleboat but had almost lost General Washington's secret letter as well. Jonathan shuddered. The captain would probably order to have him shot for treason if he ever learned that.

Perhaps he should wait, he reasoned. He needed some real proof before he talked to Captain Brewster about Bracy. Besides, if things went well on this mission, it could prove both his loyalty and his worth to the captain.

Jonathan felt better now that he had made his decision. He listened to the rhythm of the oars bumping softly against the oarlocks and watched wisps of fog ghost-dance above the water. All was peaceful on the Devil's Belt.

Gradually the rowing became more difficult. It seemed to Jonathan that the closer the *Spindrift* got to Long Island, the harder it was to push against a strong receding tide. He could not recall ever rowing against such a tide, and a nagging ache across his shoulders made him wish that they would reach shore soon. Push. Pull. Push. Pull.

The fog grew thicker and made it impossible to sight land. Jonathan gripped his oar with sweaty hands. He tried to ignore the smothery mist that hugged the boat and concentrate instead on pulling against the tide, but the old fear of the fog tugged at him stronger than the tide. A painful lump formed in his throat, and he wished fervently that they were out of the fog and back in Black Rock Harbor. It's crazy to be afraid of fog, he told himself, and he peered into it intensely, straining to see shapes that would not appear.

The air was still and close and had the strong kelpy smell of seaweed rotting in the sun. In spite of all the efforts of the crew, the *Spindrift* did not seem to be moving against the tide.

Maybe it isn't the tide at all, Jonathan thought. Maybe she's refusing to be swallowed up by this awful fog.

Jonathan pushed his oar deep into the water and felt it scrape against the bottom. An instant later there was the soft bump of the hull against the sand.

We've made it, he thought with relief. He turned toward Bracy, but before he could say a word he heard Packett cursing in the stern.

"If my guess is right, we're still a couple of miles from shore," Packett called ahead to Brewster. "We're caught in a blasted spring tide."

The groan that went up from the crew drowned out Brewster's response, and Jonathan looked at Bracy with a puzzled frown. "What's a spring tide?" he asked.

Bracy produced an embarrassed smile and shrugged. "It's kind of hard to explain, Jonny my friend," he said slowly.

"Nothing hard to explain about a spring tide," piped

up the sailor who sat behind Bracy. "Seems twice a month, at new and full moons, the tides ebb and flow a whole lot stronger than they do the rest of the time. A good spring tide can flood out the shores at high tide and suck the ocean pretty near dry at low. Guess that's what's happening to us now. We're probably stuck up on a sandbar way out from shore. Why, it can leave a ship as big as a frigate high and dry."

Even as the sailor talked, Jonathan could see the water dropping lower and lower. "But why do they call it a spring tide?" he asked. "This is summer."

"It has to do with speed, not the season of the year," answered the sailor. "You'll see for yourself in a few hours. It'll well up outa nowhere."

"That's right," said Bracy. "I've seen it myself."

The water was so low now that the weight of the swivel gun was causing the *Spindrift* to list slightly to the port side.

"All hands into the water and hold her steady," shouted Packett. "If she rolls on her side she'll founder when the tide comes up again."

"It'll be hours before high tide," said Bracy. "How much rope do we have? I've got an idea."

"There's a good-sized spool in the stern," said Packett. "Probably better than a thousand feet. Why?"

"The floor of the Sound is as full of hills and valleys as dry land," said Bracy. "For all we know, we could be sitting on a mountaintop, with deep water all around us and shore only a couple of miles away. Give me the end of the rope so that I can find my way back, and let me scout."

Jonathan shivered and peered into the fog. How could anyone have courage enough to go out into that with just a rope? he thought. He was ashamed now that he had been so quick to suspect his friend of wrong-doing. Bracy could not be a Tory. Not if he was willing to risk his life like this. Jonathan was glad that he hadn't gone to Brewster with his crazy idea.

Brewster had come to the back of the boat, and Packett was explaining Bracy's plan to him.

"What if you step into a sinkhole and drown?" Brewster demanded.

"What if we're stuck out here until sunup and can't get into Conscience Bay without being seen?" challenged Bracy.

"How well can you swim?"

"Well enough. Besides, I'll have hold of the end of the rope."

For a long moment the two men stared at each other and then Brewster snapped, "You'd better get going. Good luck."

Bracy stowed his oar and then turned to Jonathan, flashing a big smile. "Well, Jonny my friend, here's to luck for both of us."

Jonathan was suddenly tongue-tied. He wanted to tell Bracy how brave he was, but all that he could do was nod. A moment later, Bracy was gone.

"All right, men, into the water," shouted Packett.

"We've got to rock this boat in the soft mud until its bottom settles in deep enough to keep it from lying over on its side."

Jonathan and the other crewmen scrambled over the side and into the chilly water of the Devil's Belt, which was scarcely waist deep here. He watched the others put their backs against the side of the boat and heave upward with their shoulders. Jonathan tried to do the same, but every time he pushed against the *Spindrift* his feet slid forward in the slippery mud. Finally he located a rock with his foot that was large enough and embedded deeply enough to hold him, and he braced against that.

They rocked the boat back and forth until Packett gave the signal to stop. Only a few of the men whispered among themselves, but in the dense fog bits of whispers sounded like hoarse shouts. The dull thunk of the waves sounded ominous against the hull, but beyond the *Spindrift*, all was quiet. Jonathan closed his eyes and waited. It seemed impossible to be standing beside a boat in shallow water somewhere out in Long Island Sound.

A few moments later, the sound of voices caused him to look up. Packett was moving along the line of sailors, stopping and speaking to each one.

When he reached Jonathan, he smiled a rare smile and said, "Well, I don't expect you ever thought you'd be spendin' a night like this when you signed on, now did you, lad?"

"No, sir. But I'm doing fine," said Jonathan, trying to sound confident. "We'll get unstuck before long."

"Yup, but she'll surely not live up to her name tonight."

"Begging your pardon, sir, but I guess I don't exactly know what *Spindrift* means."

"I guess you wouldn't, unless you've been whaling in the North Atlantic," said Packett. "Well, you see, lad, spindrift is the spray that's swept by gale winds across the surface of the sea, and it moves pretty near faster than the eye can follow it."

"Yes, sir, I see what you mean." Packett began to move away. "Sir," Jonathan called after him. "Has Bracy Gwinnett come back yet?"

"Not yet," Packett answered sharply.

It seemed like hours since Bracy had taken the end of the rope and gone out searching for deep water. Jonathan tried to think about other things, pleasant things, but fears of the fog and for Bracy's safety began creeping in around the edges of his thoughts.

A long time later the fog began to lift, leaving an ever-widening ribbon of darkness between the murky water and the white mist above. But still the water lay at its ebb and still there was no word from Bracy. Jonathan stared into the darkness. How long was this nightmare going to last?

He heard splashing and looked up to see Packett wading toward him.

"We hauled the rope in," he said, placing a fatherly

hand on Jonathan's shoulder. Fear engulfed Jonathan so that he could not speak, but he already knew the answer to the question in his mind. "There was no sign of your friend Gwinnett. I'm sorry."

Jonathan nodded and held himself steady until Packett had gone. Then with flailing fists he lashed out at the fog as if it were a solid object that he could strike.

"No. No," he whispered, and leaned against the side of the boat.

Chapter 14

With the lifting of the fog the moon appeared and spread its silver light across the eerie seascape to the land which, to everyone's surprise, was as close as Packett had guessed. Jonathan scanned the vast tidal flat, but nothing moved. He studied each ghostly rock exhumed from the ocean's depths by the strange ebb tide, but none had the shape of a man. Bracy was gone.

Even as he looked, the flood tide suddenly came in— and with all the incredible speed that the crewman had predicted. Brewster was the first to see it. "All hands aboard," he shouted. "She's rollin' in!"

For a moment Jonathan could only stare open-mouthed at the swells that were rising like giant inch-worms behind the *Spindrift*. Frothy walls of water heaved up into the air only to come crashing down again with a deafening roar. Sea gulls screamed and took to the air in advance of the avalanche of sea. Drenched by spray, Jonathan gulped the electrified air and scrambled into the boat.

"Brace yourself!" someone shouted, and an instant later a great fist of water rammed the *Spindrift* and sent her bobbing across the surface as helplessly as a paper boat in a gale. The crew fought to steady her and to point her bow straight into the waves as she climbed each steep incline, teetered for a moment on the crest, and then plunged in a breath-catching swoop into the waiting trough.

Finally the waves subsided, disappearing as suddenly as they had come. When the rowing had eased, Jonathan sat up straight, stretched his arms skyward, and flexed his aching hands. He looked out across the water. To his amazement he saw that the tide had carried them over the flooded sandspit and into Conscience Bay. The bay was brimming at its banks, and the long fingerlike willow branches that usually tickled the surface of the water were now splayed across the top.

"We can rest on the bank until sunup," Brewster called out when the boat had been secured among the willows. "Grogin and Peters, stand watch."

Jonathan was relieved that he had not drawn watch. He could not recall when he had been so tired. He stowed his oar and sat for a moment staring across the boat at the empty place where Bracy had sat. Things would not be the same without him.

The other crewmen were already sprawled across the bank when Jonathan finally climbed ashore. He picked a spot apart from the others, stretched out, and wriggled into the sand until it fit the contours of his body. Every muscle ached, but he knew that he could not sleep.

How could I have doubted Bracy? he asked himself over and over again. Especially after he took such a chance saving my life. And he died knowing I didn't trust him, which makes it even worse.

Jonathan finally dozed just as light began to color the sky, and he awoke with a start a few minutes later.

"Barlowe," shouted the captain. "Over here."

Brewster motioned him to a tent of willows several yards past the spot where the *Spindrift* lay. Jonathan stood up slowly and brushed the sand off his clothes. The beach was deserted. The rest of the crew was out of sight.

The captain was holding a small valise. "As Major Tallmadge told you, it's extremely dangerous for you to go into Setauket now that you've been seen at close range by a whole company of lobsterbacks," he said. "But there's a message that's got to be picked up at the Roe Tavern, so that's why you'll have to wear these clothes." Brewster pushed the valise toward Jonathan and disappeared through the curtain of leaves.

A disguise, thought Jonathan. His hands trembled in anticipation as he hurriedly opened the bag and pulled the first piece of clothing from it.

"A skirt!" he shrieked. He dropped it as if it were a snake and picked gingerly through the remaining garments in the bag. Girl's clothes. All of them. How could Captain Brewster do a thing like this? He could not go into Setauket looking like a girl.

Jonathan sat down on a sturdy willow root and

scowled at the valise. This sure isn't what I thought spying would be like, he thought.

A mosquito droned in Jonathan's ear, but still he did not move. How could he put on those ridiculous things? How could he dress up like a girl?

Brewster returned a moment later, and his face clouded angrily when he saw Jonathan. "Why aren't you dressed? You have a mission to perform, Private Barlowe!"

Jonathan scrambled to his feet. Inside his head he was shouting to the captain that he would rather die than go on a mission wearing a dress. But when he opened his mouth, all that came out was "Yes, sir."

He could feel his ears turning red as he slowly picked up the skirt and pulled it over his head. Brewster leaned against a tree and glared at him as he put on the rest of the clothes. He stuck the bonnet onto his head and awkwardly tied a knot under his chin, glad that he could not see himself or know how absolutely awful he must look.

Brewster looked him up and down. "I guess you'll do," he said without conviction. "It's the same as before. Go to the Roe Tavern and ask for a package for John Bolton. Don't talk to anyone but Austin Roe. Got it?"

"Yes, sir."

"You'd better get going then. Good luck." Brewster stepped out into the open and looked up and down the beach. "All clear," he said.

Jonathan hesitated. He had to do this. He had no

choice. With a deep sigh he started to follow Brewster, but his foot came down on the hem of his skirt and sent him sprawling face first at the captain's feet.

Mercifully the captain said nothing. Jonathan got slowly to his feet, lifted the front of his skirt slightly, and headed for Setauket.

The trip into town was uneventful. In a way, Jonathan was glad. He did not want to attract any attention in this getup. Still, he was not at all sure that he liked the idea of playing the role of a girl so convincingly. He scarcely looked up as he crossed the town green and went past the fortified Presbyterian church. There would be no dawdling today.

Surprisingly few British soldiers were in town, and none of those that he passed gave him a second glance. Jonathan arrived at the Roe Tavern thankful that his mission was half over.

Austin Roe put down the pewter tankard that he was polishing and said with a smile, "Now what can I do for you, miss?" Recognizing Jonathan, his smile changed to a worried frown. Drawing him aside, Roe said, "I'll get your package and then you'd better hightail it back to the boat. Tell Captain Brewster that a British fleet under the command of General Tryon invaded and plundered New Haven yesterday, and there's talk that he plans to put the torch to every town along the Connecticut coast."

Jonathan stared after Austin Roe as he disappeared into an adjoining room. No wonder there were so few

British soldiers around today. They had gone with General Tryon to attack Connecticut. He would have to get back to the *Spindrift* as fast as he could.

The innkeeper was not gone long. When he returned, he carried a small basket. Its contents were covered by a coarse linen napkin.

"Here you are, miss," he drawled loudly. "Now run along with these rolls while they're still warm."

Jonathan grunted a thank you and slipped the basket over his arm the way a girl would do. He remembered just in time to raise the front of his skirt as he hurried toward the door. Now all he had to do was get back to Conscience Bay.

It was hard to keep from running, and Jonathan scuffed along with his head down so the bonnet would hide his face. He quickened his step as he crossed the town green. A group of boys lounged in the grass, and he lowered his head even farther as he hurried past them.

Suddenly Jonathan stopped. He had seen something out of the corner of one eye—something that he did not want to believe. He turned his head slowly toward the church. There, beside the breastworks, stood a goat hitched to a cart with a sail drooping in the still air. It was Levi Adams' cart. It had to be. There could be only one cart like that, and Levi Adams either was dead drunk in the bottom of it or else was inside the church talking to the British.

Jonathan clutched his skirt and went slowly toward the cart. He had to know.

Just then the goat spotted him, too. Stamping and

snorting softly as he came close, it followed his every step with big stern eyes. "Nice goat," whispered Jonathan. "Whoa there. I'm not going to hurt anything. I just want to look inside your wagon."

Making a wide path around the glaring goat, Jonathan eased up to the side of the cart. He waited a moment until he felt sure that the goat was not going to charge and then glanced quickly into the wagon. It was empty. Levi Adams was in the church.

Jonathan stood for a moment in stunned silence. He had been right about Levi Adams, after all. He dared not take a chance on Adams' seeing him now.

Just as he started to move away, the front doors of the fortress opened. Jonathan ducked behind the cart and peered around the edge of the sail. He could not believe what he saw. Levi Adams was coming down the steps, and beside him was Bracy Gwinnett!

Tears stung Jonathan's eyes. Bracy was alive. He had not drowned. Instead he had swum to shore to betray them all.

The two men stopped beside the breastworks, but Jonathan could not hear what they were saying. He had to run, to get away before they saw him. Jonathan looked around for some place to hide, but the breastworks were too high to jump over and all the trees stood across the road in the town green.

Bracy was gone when Jonathan looked back again, but he did not have time to wonder where. Levi Adams was heading toward his goat cart, and any second he would spy Jonathan crouching behind it.

There was only one chance. He would have to run for it. Clutching the bothersome skirt, he took a deep breath, and careened around the end of the cart. Whack! The precious basket smacked against the end of the cart spilling its contents on the ground.

Both Jonathan and Levi Adams stopped dead in their tracks, staring at each other like strange cats.

"Aha!" shrieked Adams. "It's *you*, you string-muscled, slack-shouldered, gourd-gutted, fumble-footed *brat!*"

Jonathan dodged as if to run, but stopped again and looked into the basket. It was empty. That meant that whatever important message he was carrying for General Washington was lying somewhere in the dirt.

The half dozen rolls had scattered like grapeshot, and Jonathan scrambled to retrieve them while Levi Adams lumbered toward him, cursing as he came. Adams had almost reached him when Jonathan grabbed the last roll and the linen napkin and stuffed them into the basket. Then he plunged headlong down the street.

"After him, Marmaduke. After him!" cried Adams.

Jonathan stopped for an instant to catch his breath and look behind. The goat cart was sailing down the street with canvas billowing and with Adams perched upon the driver's seat snorting and holding a whip over his head.

Chapter 15

Jonathan took off again, the basket of rolls clutched to his chest. He could not risk spilling them a second time.

People along the street stopped to stare, and others leaned out of their windows to see what was causing the commotion. A yapping terrier joined the chase for a block or two.

All at once Jonathan felt the skirt closing around his ankles, and an instant later he stumbled to his knees. As soon as he could untangle himself, he got to his feet. He had lost precious time. The cart was gaining on him.

Jonathan hiked the skirt up, dropped the basket inside the folds, and held on to the skirt as if he were carrying a tow sack. Then he was off again. Running was easier now, but the goat cart was moving surprisingly fast.

He cut through a yard and startled some chickens, who a moment later scattered every which way when the goat cart came thundering through. Jonathan darted across yard after yard. He was panting for breath, and an ache was starting in his side. If he did not stop soon, he would drop, but he could hear the goat cart getting closer and Adams cursing and cracking his whip.

Jonathan turned down a narrow street. He was near the outskirts of town now, and he could not risk leading Levi Adams to Conscience Bay and the hidden whale-boat. He had to find a place to hide.

The street was deserted, and Jonathan spun around as he tried desperately to spot a hiding place that Levi Adams would not find. The clatter of the goat cart grew louder and louder. Soon Adams would be on this street. Time was running out.

Dumping the basket of rolls behind a currant bush where they would be safe, Jonathan stepped between two houses and flattened himself against the side of one of them. The cart entered the street and slowed to a walk.

He can't figure out where I've gone, thought Jonathan. It won't slow him down for long, though. I've got to think of something fast.

With one eye on the road, he slowly inched his way backward along the side of the house. Suddenly his backside bumped against something hard. He stopped, almost afraid to look around. It was only a ladder leaning against the side of the house. A ladder! Why hadn't he thought of that before? Most people kept ladders against their houses in case of fire. He could climb up on the roof. Adams would never think of looking for him there.

Quick as a cat Jonathan scaled the ladder. He stretched out on his stomach and peered over the peak of the roof.

The goat cart was moving very slowly up the street, with its canvas sail flapping loosely in the breeze. From the driver's seat Adams scanned every house, tree, and bush, and muttered to himself.

The cart creaked to a halt directly in front of the house on which Jonathan was perched.

"All right. I know you're around here somewhere, you squint-eyed, slick-faced brat!" Adams flicked his whip, and the goat started moving up the street again, this time slower than ever.

He's not going to give up easily, thought Jonathan. If he turns around and comes back, he'll see me for sure.

Jonathan pulled the skirt above his knees and crawled toward the chimney that rose from the center of the roof. Perhaps he could hide behind it. Behind it? he thought. I'll hide *in* it.

He would have to do it now while Adams' back was still to him, so he stood up, leaned over the edge of the chimney, and peered into the blackness below. A moment later he was over the side, moving down slowly as he found toeholds in the bricks. Soon only his head and arms were above the lip of the chimney.

Jonathan watched Levi Adams turn his cart around and start down the street once more. Then he moved carefully to one corner of the chimney and braced his legs against the opposite corner. He ducked his head, leaving only his hands outside feeling secure enough to stay there all day if he had to.

Jonathan leaned his forehead against the bricks and looked down. Patches of light in the dark tunnel below showed where fireplaces in various rooms opened into the huge central chimney. The largest patch of light was at the bottom, where smoke would rise from the big kitchen hearth as soon as it was time to cook the evening meal.

He tightened his grip on the chimney edge and closed his eyes. Surely Levi Adams would be gone by then. He had to get the message about General Tryon's attack on Connecticut to Captain Brewster. Austin Roe had said that it was urgent. But how could he ever explain to the captain why it had taken him so long to get back?

Gradually the creaking of the goat cart died away. Jonathan waited a long time after the last sounds had faded before he raised his head above the sill and looked around. Had Adams given up and gone away? Or was he hiding now, waiting to ambush Jonathan when he tried to leave?

Nothing stirred in the warm summer air. The street was deserted once more. Slowly Jonathan pulled himself out of the chimney and onto the roof again. He looked in every direction, but there was no sign of Levi Adams anywhere.

Jonathan's dress and bonnet were covered with black soot. He pulled them off as soon as he reached the ground, glad to be rid of them. He pulled the basket of rolls from its hiding place behind the currant bush and replaced it with the bundle of girl's clothing. That was something else that he would have to explain to the captain, but, he thought with a smile, it was worth it just to have the skirt off.

He moved down the street with caution, fearful that at any moment Levi Adams would spring out at him. There was no sign of either Adams or his goat cart, and Jonathan quickened his pace as he headed for Old Field Road and Conscience Bay.

It was late afternoon when he reached the willow-lined shore. Brewster had apparently been watching for him, because he met Jonathan halfway up the hill.

"Captain Brewster," said Jonathan before the captain had a chance to speak. "Austin Roe gave me an urgent message for you. He said that a British fleet commanded by General Tryon raided New Haven yesterday, and he's heard talk that they plan to burn down every town along the Connecticut coast."

"What!" cried Brewster. He was thoughtful for a moment. Then, pointing to the basket of rolls, he asked, "Is that the package for John Bolton?"

"Yes, sir," said Jonathan. He handed Brewster the basket, knowing that he still had some explaining to do. "I guess you're wondering about my clothes. Well, I wore that girl's stuff into town like I was supposed to and everything, but on the way back I had a little trouble and they got awfully messed up. I thought I'd be more noticeable wearing them than not, so I rolled them up and hid them behind a bush."

Brewster regarded him solemnly for a moment and

then snapped, "We'll discuss it later, Private. Now get into the boat."

Brewster summoned Packett, and a few minutes later the two men climbed aboard the *Spindrift* and called all hands together in the bow. The captain repeated the message that Jonathan had given him and then went on.

"If my information is right, we may be heading into trouble, but we're on an important mission and we've got to take the chance. Instead of Black Rock Harbor, we'll head west of there toward Mill River. There are a lot of creeks and sloughs along that part of the shore that'll hide us pretty well—that's if we can make it through without being spotted by the warships."

There was mumbling among the men, but no one spoke up with an objection.

"Load your muskets and prepare to cast off," Packett ordered. "We should be across about an hour past sunset."

Jonathan loaded his Brown Bess and set his oar in its lock. What would they find on the other side of the Devil's Belt? Perhaps they would get into battle after all.

The crew rowed in silence across the churning water, pulling their oars with the extra measure of strength that comes with fear. Most of them had families in Fairfield and the surrounding countryside. Their wives and children were alone now, defenseless, and the men moved the *Spindrift* across the Devil's Belt at a speed that matched her name.

At first the Connecticut shoreline was a gray vapor that blended indistinguishably with the water of the Sound. But soon, as the evening shadows lengthened, Jonathan could see smoke smudging the sky, billowing higher and higher, and spreading wider and wider. Fairfield was on fire!

As darkness fell, the masts of three British frigates appeared silhouetted against the tawny red glow.

"They're anchored off Kensie's Point," Packett shouted from the stern. "They shouldn't have much crew aboard, and what's there will be watching the shore. If we wait for more darkness and give them a good wide berth, we should be able to slip into Mill River without being seen."

Jonathan hoped with all his heart that Packett was right.

"Still your oars and keep low. Let her drift with the tide. Pass the word," came a hoarse whisper at Jonathan's back.

He passed it on and listened as little by little the rhythmic thud of the oars gave way to stillness and the gentle lapping of waves against the *Spindrift*'s hull. Jonathan cocked his musket and slid off his seat and onto his knees so that only his eyes were above the side of the boat. He fought back a wave of fear and looked at the other crewmen, who like himself were crouched in the boat, tensely watching and waiting for the first sign of danger. Nevertheless, he did not know when he had ever felt so totally alone.

The smell of smoke was heavy in the air as the *Spindrift* floated across the water. They were close enough to one of the ships for Jonathan to see the dark outline of a sentry on deck, but just as Packett had predicted, his attention was on the beach and the blazing town beyond.

When the whaleboat reached the mouth of Mill River, Packett ordered the crew to row, and soon they were out of sight of the beach and tucked safely into an inlet a quarter of a mile upriver from the Sound. Jonathan breathed a sigh of relief and changed the cock on his Brown Bess to the safety position. The danger had passed, at least for now.

He did not have long to rest. "Barlowe," called Brewster a moment later. In the darkness Jonathan could barely make out a small roll of paper in the captain's hand. He handed it to Jonathan as soon as he approached. "This is the message that you got from Austin Roe today, and it must reach Major Tallmadge tonight. The countryside will be crawling with lobsterbacks. You're the only one among us who'll have a chance of getting through."

Jonathan could not believe what he had heard. Not only was the captain trusting him to carry a secret message through enemy-infested territory, he had also said that Jonathan was the only one who could do it. He had finally proved himself. The captain knew that he was a man.

"Yes, sir," said Jonathan, stuffing the message inside his shirt. "And don't worry, sir. I'll get through. You can count on it."

"Follow Mill River north until you come to Kings Highway. Go west toward Norwalk. The major is camped on the outskirts of the town. Any questions?"

"No, sir."

Brewster reached out a huge hand and gave Jonathan's hand a hearty shake. "Then good luck."

Chapter 16

A chorus of frogs stopped their concert as Jonathan hopped out of the *Spindrift* and onto the bank. The countryside was peaceful. Except for the faint smoky smell, it was hard to imagine that only a few miles beyond the trees an entire town was aflame.

He made his way quickly to Mill River and found close to the bank a grassy trail that was easy to follow. The moon sparkled in the softly rippling water, and night birds called to each other in the trees. All of the fears of the past few hours were gone, and Jonathan struck an easy gait as he headed north.

In the solitude of the woods he could not help but think about Bracy Gwinnett, the man he had thought was his friend. He was almost certain that Bracy and Zeke were the Tories who had escaped from Newgate Prison. They had to be. It all fit together now. Why else would Bracy have wanted to hide Zeke's body where no one would ever find it? And why else would he have wanted to set up a spy operation with Levi Adams?

Bracy had been Levi's partner. He knew that now. And they had planned to spy on Brewster's whaleboat navy and report what they found to the British in Setauket. That was why the British soldiers had attacked the *Spindrift* in Conscience Bay.

Jonathan winced. It hurt to have someone make a fool of you the way Bracy had made a fool of him. But how was one to know whom to trust and whom not to trust? he thought. People like Levi Adams were easy. They almost told you themselves. But it was different with people like Bracy Gwinnett.

Jonathan stopped and skipped a couple of stones across the surface of the water. It would be nice if he could sit down for a few minutes and enjoy the peaceful scene, but Brewster had entrusted him with a mission, and there was no time to waste. He moved on down the trail whistling a tune.

"Halt. State your name and where you're going."

Jonathan froze as a British soldier stepped out of the shadows and straddled the path directly ahead of him. Jonathan turned to run, but another redcoat blocked the path behind him.

"Jonathan . . . Jonathan Barlowe," he stammered. "I'm on my way home."

"Where have you been?" demanded the first soldier.

Jonathan cleared his throat and tried to think of an answer.

"Well?"

"I've been down at the beach. I was . . . I was watch-

ing the ships anchored off Kensie's Point." Jonathan held his breath. What if they didn't believe him? What if they searched him and found the rolled-up letter hidden inside his shirt?

"Where do you live?" asked the soldier behind him.

Jonathan's mind raced. He had never been along this part of Mill River before, so he did not know whether there were any houses nearby. "Up on Kings Highway," he said, feeling certain that there would be houses there. "I'd better get going, too. It's late, and my folks'll be worried."

The first soldier stepped aside and gestured for Jonathan to pass. "Get going," he mumbled.

Jonathan tried to hold his knees steady as he went forward. He had seen the man before. He was the red-haired private who had found him hiding in the bushes the day he shot off the British cannon.

Jonathan ducked his head as he went by, but he was not quick enough.

"Hey! Wait!"

Jonathan took off at a run. He could hear the redcoats coming behind him.

"Hey! You're the lad who set off the cannon," yelled the soldier who had allowed him to pass. "Come back here!"

Jonathan plunged into the undergrowth. He could stay on the path and try to outrun them, but that might not work. His best bet would be to lose them—if he could—somewhere in the dense tangle of thicket and trees. Jonathan ran blindly through the dark woods with only an occasional splash of moonlight to light his way. Once he stopped and listened over the pounding of his heart. They were still coming, crashing through the underbrush straight in his direction.

On he ran, stumbling among tree roots, tripping over rocks, until exhaustion forced him to stop in a clearing and catch his breath. He leaned against a tree and gulped air. He could hear the soldiers coming closer and closer. Frantically Jonathan looked around. He was too tired to go on. He would have to hide. But where?

The branches were out of reach on the tree that he leaned against, and the other trees nearby were mostly saplings, neither tall nor strong enough to climb. There was only one other possibility, and the thought made Jonathan cringe. Beside him was a mound of bramble bushes. He stuck out a finger and touched the saberlike point of one of the thorns. The British soldiers would never look for him there.

Jonathan hesitated. He could already feel the brambles scratching at his skin. But the sound of the approaching redcoats was growing louder, and suddenly the words of Major Tallmadge flashed into his mind. "The next morning he was hanged without benefit of a trial or the comfort of a Bible. Nathan Hale was only nineteen."

He was caught carrying intelligence information, thought Jonathan. Just like I'm doing now. He dropped to the ground, gritted his teeth against the pain, and backed slowly under the bush. The thorns tore at his flesh and tangled painfully in his hair, but Jonathan kept on scooting until he was well out of sight.

An instant later the redcoats were in the clearing. Jonathan could hear them panting breathlessly.

"Listen," one of them said. "I don't hear him anymore. He's probably hiding somewhere."

"Either that, or he's got away," said the other.

The men rested no more than three feet from where Jonathan lay hidden. The pain from the thorns was growing worse, and he could feel drops of blood trickling down his sides. Why were they stopping for so long? Why didn't they move on?

"Let's round up some of the others. We can fan out and cover more territory that way."

"Good idea. We'd better get moving."

The two soldiers headed back in the same direction that they had come from. Jonathan did not move for a long time after the sound of their footsteps had died away. He had to be sure they were really gone. Finally he pulled himself out from under the bramble bush and stood up on unsteady legs. The scratches on his back stung with pain, but he dared not stay in the clearing any longer. He had to move on.

The going was slower now, but before long he found the path beside the river again, and he pushed on as fast as his smarting back would allow. It was impossible to calculate how long it would take the two soldiers to find the rest of their party and start after him again. His legs felt as heavy as tree stumps as he plodded along the twisting trail.

All of a sudden he stopped. He had heard something. He was sure of it.

Jonathan listened. The river splashed and gurgled and somewhere an owl screeched. He tiptoed forward, straining to catch the slightest sound. There it was again, a squeaking, creaking sort of sound, and it came from the direction where he was heading.

Holding his breath, Jonathan crept on along the path. He could not turn back. He had to find out what was making the noise. There was a chance that it was more British soldiers, but it might also be someone who could help him.

The path slowly widened into a clearing that reached all the way down to the river. There at the water's edge stood an old mill with stone walls overgrown with moss and vines. It looked forlorn standing in the silver moonlight. Its windows were boarded shut, and its rickety mill wheel moaned softly in the breeze.

That must have been the sound I heard, thought Jonathan with a sigh of relief. The mill looked as if it had been deserted for a long time. Perhaps he could rest there for a little while.

Jonathan caught the scent of tobacco as he walked up to the door and pushed aside the vines that covered a small sign hanging nearby. "Hogan's Snuff Mill," it said. He had heard that Mill River had been named after the many mills that dotted its banks. This must be one of them, he thought.

Leaning against the door, Jonathan looked longingly toward the river. If only he could bathe his cuts in the cool water and rest for a few minutes—then he could outrun the entire British army. He was sure of it. Perhaps if he hurried he would have time.

Suddenly he heard the sound of voices. They were faint and far away, but they were voices, men's voices —there was no mistaking that. They were coming from the same direction that he had just come. It must be the redcoats, he thought. They'll be here any second.

Jonathan looked around desperately. He saw no place to hide in the moonswept clearing that surrounded the snuff mill, and if he started to run again they would hear him. There was only one thing for him to do.

Jonathan tugged at the door to the mill. The hinges were rusty and stubborn, and it took all his strength to open it far enough to squeeze inside. A thin knife of moonlight stabbed the darkness from the open door, but as soon as he pushed the door shut again the room was pitch black once more. Fine tobacco dust rose in the air and tickled his nose with each step. He held his breath as he felt his way along the wall. When he reached the corner he stopped, waited a moment for the tobacco dust to settle, and listened. The voices were growing louder. They were charging up the path straight for the clearing and the mill.

Jonathan shook his head in the darkness. He should never have hidden in the mill. They would be sure to look inside. The darkness was the only hope he had. Even if they came in, perhaps they would not see him.

"Look at this old mill."

The soldiers were in the clearing. Jonathan flattened himself against the wall. Suddenly he remembered the rolled-up letter for General Washington inside his shirt. He could not risk being caught with that.

Jonathan drew the paper from inside his shirt and dropped to his knees without a sound. He pushed the letter deep into the corner, but as he did another cloud of snuff rose into the air. At least the letter would be safe even if he was not, he reasoned, rubbing his twitching nose.

He could hear the soldiers milling around outside. "This place looks pretty well boarded up to me," said one of them.

Jonathan felt a sneeze growing inside his head. The soldiers were moving away from the mill. He clamped both hands over his nose and mouth. His eyes were stinging and he choked to hold his breath. If only they would move faster. If only they would run.

"Ah . . . ah . . . ah . . . choooo!"

Chapter 17

All the while he was being marched along Kings Highway toward Fairfield by his captors, Jonathan's mind was on the message for General Washington that he had hidden inside the old snuff mill. Captain Brewster was counting on him to deliver it to Major Tallmadge tonight. He could not let the captain down. Somehow he would have to escape.

But how? He was being led to town by six musket-toting British soldiers, and one of the muskets was pointed squarely at his back. He could only hope that in the confusion of the blazing town he would get his chance.

Kings Highway was the main road in and out of Fairfield, and as they neared the town they were met by a swirling mass of terrified people. Many had been routed out of their beds by the rapidly spreading flames, and they were half naked. The tawny red reflecting on their sweaty bodies and the horror on their faces gave them the look of scampering demons. Crying children were being jerked along unmercifully by panic-stricken parents, who were burdened with all the household goods that they could carry.

Jonathan searched the faces of the people as they streamed past. Surely someone would notice what had happened to him and help him escape.

But all of them were too intent on saving themselves to pay attention to him. Ahead, the fire rose like a crimson backdrop to the drama. The deep-red base blended upward into pink flecked with black as tinderbox houses exploded in a holocaust of sparks and flung their charred timbers into the air. Black smoke, somber as a parson's hat, blotted out the sky.

As they entered the streets of Fairfield, the crash of falling roofs and the roar and crackle of the flames mingled with the shouts of red-coated soldiers, who burst forth from every direction like sparks from the blaze.

"Bring the torch!"

"Fire this one!"

But they were not alone in their destruction. Jonathan watched in horror as a fighting cock with its beautiful plumes aflame flew screeching from rooftop to rooftop, igniting every shingle, sill, and cupola that it touched.

New walls of fire sprang up at every turn. Heat seared Jonathan's nostrils and smoke stung his eyes and made him cough. Where could they possibly be taking him? Why were they marching him straight into the heart of town?

When they reached the village green, the soldiers led him to a group of officers who stood talking together.

Jonathan recognized the one who stepped forward in spite of a large black smudge across his cheek. He was the captain who had led the attack on the *Spindrift*, and his eyes widened in surprise when he saw Jonathan.

"Well, look whom we have here," he said in his clipped British accent. "The young rogue who shot off my cannon. Don't tell me you're playing spy again?"

Jonathan stiffened and met the captain's gaze, but he did not say a word. He would never talk. They could not make him.

"We found him near the river, sir," said the red-haired private proudly. "We were sure that he was up to no good, so we chased him down."

"I presume that you searched him?"

"Yes, sir. The moment we caught him."

"And you found nothing?" asked the captain.

"No, sir," said the private.

"Good work, men. Jordan, you and Sterling put him in a rowboat and take him out to the ship for now. I'll question him later."

Hands were clamped around both of Jonathan's arms as a soldier stepped up on either side of him and prepared to lead him away. Jonathan knew that once he was aboard a British ship, escape would be impossible. He had to do something now, before it was too late. He looked around frantically. Where was the home guard? Where were the soldiers from Black Rock Fort? He had not heard a shot fired since he entered the flaming town. Was no one left to make a stand?

Jonathan fought to break away from his captors, but

their grips were firm and they half dragged him toward Beach Road and the warships anchored in the Sound.

Suddenly from behind came the thunder of galloping hooves and the wild neighing of half-crazed horses. Jonathan jerked around and saw a team, nostrils flaring and legs flying, pulling a flaming wagon. They were bearing down fast, and the two British soldiers dived for cover, leaving Jonathan standing alone in the middle of the street.

There was no time to think. Jonathan propelled himself down the street ahead of the runaway team. He stretched his legs as far as he could, but the horses quickly gained on him. Finally he plunged into the grass beside the road and rolled to safety behind a tree.

Just then the crumbling chimney of a nearby house came crashing down on the wagon, splintering it to bits. One horse fell, but the other tore loose from its harness, tossed his mane wildly, and raced toward the beach.

Jonathan lay still for a moment. So far there was no sign of the two soldiers. He hurried to the side of the fallen animal, which was still struggling to get to its feet.

"Whoa there. Whoa there, boy," said Jonathan, tugging on the stubborn harness. In a moment he had the horse free. "Come on, boy. Let me ride you," he coaxed as the animal scrambled to its feet. It eyed Jonathan for an instant and then galloped down the street out of sight.

With a sigh Jonathan looked after the fleeing horse. I

might as well head that way, too, he thought. I certainly can't go back to the center of the town.

He dodged storms of embers and bursting showers of sparks as he ran in the direction of the beach. At least he was free. It would be safer to cut across the beach and head up Mill River again than to try to go back the way he had come. He had no idea what time it was, but he was sure that morning was not far off, and he still had a long way to go.

Soon the blazing town was behind him, and Jonathan slowed to a walk as he got close to the beach. He was tired and the scratches on his back still hurt, but he knew that he had to keep on going. If only he had been able to catch one of the runaway horses. How much faster he would have been able to complete his mission! And how much easier it would have been to get away if he should happen to meet another party of British soldiers.

As if in answer to his thoughts, a soft whinny came from somewhere to his right. Jonathan looked up. There on a sandy rise in the moonlight were the two horses munching on tufts of beach grass.

Jonathan crept quietly toward the animals. They seemed calm enough. Surely this time, if he talked softly and did not rush them, he would be able to mount one.

"Whoa there. Whoa, fellows," said Jonathan. He reached out a hand to stroke the neck of the nearest horse. The animal neighed nervously and backed away, but the other one continued to nibble contentedly on the grass. Jonathan stood still and talked to it in soft, coaxing tones. He would have to do this right. He could not take any chances on spooking this one. He needed it too badly.

The broken reins hung from the bridle and dangled in the sand. Jonathan reached for it and wrapped the end around his hand. Then he moved cautiously toward the animal once more. The horse stopped eating and looked at Jonathan, but it did not seem to be afraid. Slowly Jonathan ran his hand down the horse's neck. "Easy, boy," he whispered. "Easy there. I'm not going to hurt you."

The animal nuzzled against Jonathan's chest. It's now or never, he thought, and he leaped onto the horse's bare back. The animal responded to the slap of the reins and an instant later was racing swiftly over the sand.

At the mouth of Mill River, Jonathan turned north. He passed several small inlets, knowing that in one of them Captain Brewster was probably pacing up and down in the *Spindrift*, anxiously awaiting his return. He intended to make it this time, even though he would be a little later than expected.

The letter for General Washington was in the corner of the snuff mill just where Jonathan had left it. He held his nose as he entered the mill and retrieved the message quickly.

He stopped outside only long enough to let the horse drink from the river. Then on he went, spurring the horse to breakneck speed. Jonathan forgot his tiredness and the painful scratches on his back. All he could think about was the letter inside his shirt and the moment when he would hand it to Major Tallmadge.

The first rays of dawn were streaking the sky as Jonathan reached the encampment of Light Dragoons. A pair of sentries paced back and forth before the entrance to the camp.

"Who goes there?" shouted one of them as Jonathan approached.

"Private Jonathan Barlowe of the Continental Artillery," he answered proudly.

"Why are you out of uniform, Private?"

"I'm on a special mission and I have to see Major Tallmadge right away."

The sentry studied Jonathan carefully for a minute and then said, "What say you to 'virtue'?"

"I don't know the answer to your password, sir. But if you'll tell Major Tallmadge that I've been sent by Captain Caleb Brewster, I'm sure he'll want to see me."

With a sigh the sentry turned and headed toward Major Tallmadge's marquee. The other sentry resumed his pacing. Jonathan slid off his lathered horse and stroked its side, glancing nervously toward the major's marquee from time to time.

The sentry returned on the double. "The major will see you. Follow me."

Jonathan's heart was pounding as he ducked under the flap of the tent. He marched quickly to the major's desk.

Major Tallmadge looked up from his work and

smiled. "I'm glad to see that you were able to get through, Private Barlowe. Now what do you have for me?"

"A package for John Bolton, sir," said Jonathan with a grin. Reaching inside his shirt, he pulled out the roll of paper and handed it to the major.

Slowly Major Tallmadge unrolled the precious message. Jonathan stared down at it in horror. The sheet of paper was blank.

Chapter 18

Jonathan could not believe his eyes. It was impossible to think that he had risked his life for a piece of paper with nothing on it.

Major Tallmadge rolled the paper up again and got slowly to his feet. He went to his campaign chest and drew out a small brush and a vial of liquid.

"Don't be alarmed, Private," he said, as if he had read Jonathan's thoughts. "Your risk was not for nothing."

The major returned to his desk and looked at Jonathan solemnly for a moment before he spoke again. "Draw up a stool. You are a trusted and important member of this operation, and there are some things that you have a right to know."

Jonathan pulled a camp stool up to the desk and sat down. He was anxious to hear what the major had to say.

"First, I think you should know that I am John Bolton. That is my code name, just as Samuel Culper is the code name for our man in New York. But that is just one of our secrets."

As he talked, Major Tallmadge unrolled the paper again and spread it across his desk. Then he uncorked the vial and dipped the brush into the colorless liquid.

"Watch what happens when I brush this across your piece of blank paper."

Jonathan leaned closer to the desk and watched tensely. Guided by Major Tallmadge's hand, the brush sailed back and forth across the page, leaving in its wake line after line of finely drawn numbers. Jonathan stared at the paper in openmouthed surprise.

"This was written with Sympathetic Stain," explained the major. "It's a type of ink that becomes invisible when it dries. The liquid in this vial is the only substance that will bring it back into view."

Jonathan whistled low. Code names. Invisible ink. He was involved in something far larger than he had ever imagined.

"As you can see," the major went on, "the message is written in code. Each of these figures stands for a word. I decipher the code and then pass the message on to General Washington."

"Do the British have Sympathetic Stain, too?" asked Jonathan.

"No, but they know that we have it, and they're very anxious to capture a sample to be analyzed. Perhaps now you understand how really important your missions were, even though at times they seemed a little strange to you."

Jonathan nodded with a grin, thinking that there must

be words which could express how proud and happy he felt, if only he could find them. He had never—not even in his wildest dreams—imagined anything like this. And he, Jonathan Barlowe, had been right in the middle of the whole thing.

"I know that you need rest," Major Tallmadge went on. "And I would ordinarily ask you to stay here until General Washington's reply is ready for you to carry back across the Devil's Belt on its way to Samuel Culper in New York. However, I've had word that the British plan to attack Norwalk next, and you would be in grave danger here. I'll see that you have a fresh horse to take you back to the whaleboat, and I'll bring the General's message to you myself."

Jonathan hesitated a moment and then looked Major Tallmadge squarely in the eye. "I appreciate your telling me all this. But there's something that you need to know." He paused to choose his words and then went on, "I can't ever go back into Setauket, sir. You'll have to find someone to take my place as a spy."

"What!" said Major Tallmadge. "What do you mean?"

"There was a member of Captain Brewster's crew named Bracy Gwinnett who enlisted the same night I did. He said that he was a fisherman and that he and his partner Zeke were caught in a storm out on the Sound and that Zeke was killed. Anyway, the last time we took the *Spindrift* across we got left high and dry by a spring tide about two miles from the Long Island shore. Bracy went looking for deep water and never came back. We all thought he'd drowned, but then I saw him yesterday in Setauket and he was coming out of the British headquarters in the Presbyterian church."

"Does he know that you're a spy?"

"No, sir, but he might suspect. He knows that Captain Brewster always sends me into town."

Major Tallmadge leaned back in his chair with a sigh and lapsed into thought. Jonathan could relax now. He was glad that the truth about Bracy Gwinnett was finally out, even though he had not told the whole story. Perhaps he would never have to tell anyone about Levi Adams and the disaster that had almost happened because of him. But being free and independent meant making decisions on his own, and he had found out firsthand that it was not always easy to know what was the right thing to do. I suppose that if this country gets her independence, she'll have that problem, too, he mused.

Finally Major Tallmadge leaned forward in his chair. "Private Barlowe," he said, with a twinkle flickering in his eyes. "I have thought this over and I agree that you cannot continue as a spy, but I consider Captain Brewster's loss to be my gain. I shall see to it that you are transferred to the Second Regiment of Light Dragoons as my personal orderly."

Jonathan was speechless. "Thank you, sir. Thank you!" was all that he could say.

The British had left Fairfield, and for the next few weeks, while he waited for his reassignment to become official, Jonathan worked helping the people of the town clear away the debris that had once been their homes, so they could start the long and difficult task of rebuilding. He was anxious to begin his new duties, and the days seemed to drag by until one afternoon he looked up from his work to see a soldier approaching on horseback. He was wearing the uniform of the Light Dragoons, and as he came near he called out: "Are you Private Jonathan Barlowe?"

"Yes, sir," said Jonathan, snapping to attention.

The soldier dismounted and faced Jonathan squarely. "I have a message from Major Tallmadge," he said. "You are to be in the town green tomorrow morning at ten o'clock sharp."

"I'll be there," said Jonathan without hesitation, but he was puzzled. Why would Major Tallmadge want to see him in the town green? Why not at his camp?

Jonathan wanted to ask the soldier who had brought the order, but he had already mounted his horse again and started back up the street.

Sleep did not come easily that night. Jonathan could not get the mysterious message from Major Tallmadge out of his mind. Over and over he wondered why the major had chosen the green, which had become the town meeting place since the church had been destroyed in the fire. Finally he drifted off to sleep and was awakened the next morning by the sound of clapping boards.

Jonathan dressed quickly and hurried to the green. Why were the townspeople being summoned? What did it have to do with him? People were streaming in from all directions. Some stood in groups under the trees.

Others sat on the grass. Major Tallmadge was near the center of the green. The Light Dragoons stood in marching formation nearby.

When the major saw Jonathan, he motioned to him. Smiling broadly, he said, "This is a day that you're not likely to forget for a long time, Private Barlowe."

"Why?" asked Jonathan in surprise. "What's going to happen?"

"Stay nearby. You'll find out very soon," replied the major.

Jonathan was puzzled, but soon the last stragglers had found their way onto the green. Major Tallmadge asked for silence to address the crowd.

"Ladies and gentlemen," he began. "It is my privilege to call you here today to publicly honor a young man for extraordinary service to his country. The young man is here beside me. He is Private Jonathan Barlowe of the Continental Artillery."

Jonathan could feel his ears turning red as Major Tallmadge continued to speak. "On the night of July 7, 1779, the same night that Fairfield was attacked and burned, Private Barlowe singlehandedly escaped from capture by the enemy. Although he was injured and was near exhaustion, he completed a mission of extreme importance and secrecy. Our commander in chief, General Washington, has ordered that when any singularly meritorious action is performed, the author shall be permitted to wear on his facings over his left breast the figure of a heart in purple cloth. The soldier's name and the account of his deed shall be entered in the Book of

Merit, and he may pass all guards and sentinels by whom officers may pass."

General Tallmadge paused and turned to Jonathan. "Private Barlowe, by order of General Washington, I present to you the Purple Heart."

In Major Tallmadge's outstretched hand was a heart of purple silk with a narrow edge of lace. Jonathan stared at it in silence, trying to comprehend the words that the major had just spoken. He barely heard the cheers of the crowd.

"Here. Take it. It won't bite," said the major with a smile as he pushed the heart into Jonathan's hand. "Your reassignment has come through. Report to camp first thing in the morning. And one more thing: Captain Brewster sends his congratulations. He was sorry that he couldn't be here today."

Jonathan nodded. He wanted to speak, but the words were still stuck in his throat. Somehow he felt that Major Tallmadge understood.

People were pressing around him, shaking his hand and wishing him well. Dozens of little boys stuck out grimy fingers to touch the beautiful Purple Heart.

Finally Jonathan ducked through the crowd and headed for the deserted beach. He looked out across the Devil's Belt wondering if at that moment the *Spindrift* was hiding in the willows at Conscience Bay and if someone else was hurrying into Setauket on the special business that he had grown to love. After a while he headed back toward town. Even though my spy career is over, things have turned out pretty well, he thought as he sauntered along. Especially since at first my fate seemed to be nothing but disaster.

Suddenly his foot struck a rock, which sent him sprawling face first on the ground. With a disgusted sigh he raised himself up on one elbow and looked around. The beautiful badge lay nearby covered with dirt. Jonathan got to his feet and retrieved the Purple Heart, carefully brushing it clean. Then he raised his head high, squared his shoulders, and marched on up the street whistling a tune.

Author's Note

Today you can still see colonial homes that were spared when the British burned Fairfield, Connecticut, on July 7, 1779. Across Long Island Sound in Setauket, the Presbyterian church continues to stand on the village green, and there is a marker at the site of the Roe Tavern. For Austin Roe and Major Benjamin Tallmadge really existed, and they acted out their roles in General Washington's espionage ring just as they are portrayed here, passing messages written in the mysterious Sympathetic Stain.

Caleb Brewster and the whaleboat navy also were a real part of America's past, but Jonathan Barlowe, Bracy Gwinnett, and Levi Adams are fictional figures created by the author's imagination. But who can say for certain that there never was a boy much like Jonathan who rode the waves in a whaleboat as a spy on the Devil's Belt?